Closing the Gap
& Other Stories

John Mack

2014 © John Mack   www.johnmack.co.nz

ISBN 978-0-9941011-2-9 [paperback]
ISBN 978-0-9941011-3-6 [ebook]

Editor: Jenny Argante
Cover Painting: Mary McTavish *Closing the Gap*
Printed By: Printing.Com

The Little Red Hen
Community Press
PO Box 13-533
Tauranga Central 3141
New Zealand

Closing the Gap
& Other Stories

For Mary

Contents

Closing the Gap

There was nobody to see them off: no wives, no girlfriends, no mothers nor grandmothers. No fathers, no sons nor uncles. Apart from the dockhand manning the hawsers there was no one there.

There was no fanfare for their departure; unlike for the cruise ships or even the big freighters. Sometimes the company agent was there with last minute instructions, but not today as it was Sunday. The docks were quiet: machinery idle, cranes still, forklifts silent. A few gulls strutted about, squatters in temporary occupation before the working week began again.

Tony, Seaswirl's skipper, felt their departure deserved some sort of recognition. Even though he had made departures like this hundreds of times before, it saddened him that it went unnoticed. Part of his job as captain was to shoulder the responsibility for bringing his crew and vessel safely home.

He knew that far out at sea beyond sight of land, beyond any hope of swift help, at the limit of radio contact, a moment's inattention could mean terrible injury from being caught in the winches, concussed by the swinging gear, decapitated by lashing wire rope, scalded by hot water in the galley or dragged overboard by the setting nets to death by drowning.

Or simply sickness.

This was the most difficult time of any voyage; that transition between life on land and life at sea. Still tied to the conventions and bewilderments of their land life, the crew were morose and taciturn; going about their tasks automatically in preparation for casting off. Had there been even one loved one, one friend, one relative or even an interested bystander they would have adopted a jaunty devil-may-care attitude that would have carried them until they were at sea and their small ship-bound society became their whole world.

Tony allowed his thoughts to drift as the crew bustled around him. He imagined that the woman, whom even now he thought of as his wife, was sitting down to lunch in a sunny clean room of a sprawling house overlooking green hills with the sea in the distance. The house in his imaginings bore a resemblance to the home they had shared before the divorce.

That had been five years ago and Tony had heard that she had remarried. But he couldn't let the idea of her go and often realised, usually with a self-admonitory start, that he was a fool to think of her at all, let alone wish that things could ever again be as they once were. He wasn't sure the shadowy man joining his wife at the dining table in his fantasy was him.

"Just about ready to go, Skipper," reported Jimbo, his first mate.

Tony nodded.

"Get Rob to call up the Harbour Master and let him know we'll be moving at the top of the tide."

He knew Jimbo would have done that anyway, but he needed to give some response to show Jimbo, and himself, that his mind was on the job.

There were eleven in the crew of Seaswirl. Besides Tony there was Jimbo, the first mate; Rob, the radio and electronics officer; Woody, the engineer and his assistant, Jim; Cooky, the cook and his assistant, Roger, and the four deckhands: Tiger, Billy, Samson and Junior. The deckhands and assistants to the engineer and cook came and went with each voyage rotating through the company fleet or away to an easier life.

Of the crew he knew Jimbo best. A giant of a man, more than capable of captaining a vessel the size of Seaswirl, in line for the next company vacancy that came up. Jimbo rarely had need to raise his voice or use his size to intimidate; the deckhands responded to an authority born of experience and confidence.

In charge of the engine room and all things mechanical was Woody. He was the opposite of Jimbo in stature and character. Small and wiry, balding with a greasy bushy beard, he had plenty to say about everything and anything. Still, it kept them entertained around the dinner table for the first few nights at sea, before it became irritating.

Rob, the radio operator and their electronic guru, kept pretty much to himself. He also acted as second mate and had watch-keeping duties along with Tony and Jimbo. Off duty, with the radios and radar set on automatic alarm, Rob would hibernate in his cabin, earphones clamped to his head, listening to melancholy new age music. Tony had half jokingly banned playing the music over the ship's loudspeakers for fear the crew would mutiny in a rush of self-pitying loneliness.

Cooky, whose real name was Ted, flounced around like a fairy queen. That didn't matter to Tony as long as it didn't bother the crew. At times when they were trawling round the clock, sometimes in big seas when Seaswirl rolled and pitched enough to make standing up tricky, Tony considered Cooky the most important man on the ship as he kept hot meals and hot drinks coming in an endless stream from the galley.

"Time to go, Skipper."

Jimbo's soft voice came over the bridge speaker.

Tony looked out the wheelhouse window to the foc'sle where Jimbo stood, RT in hand, directing the mooring party. He sighed and, forcing himself back in the present, dismissed all from his mind but the task in front of him.

He leant forward and spoke into the mike.

"Cast off forward," he said, and watched for Jimbo's waved acknowledgement.

The incoming tide caught the bow and slowly pushed it away from the dock at the same moment Tony rang up 'slow ahead port' on the engine room telegraph.

As the big twin diesels rumbled deep within the ship he watched Jimbo stride after the deckhands as they ran towards the stern. The thrust from the port engine held the bow against the push of the tide. The only link left with the land was the stern hawser.

Tony, judging his moment, called into the mike, "Ready when you are, Jimbo, let go aft."

Watching from the wing of the bridge, Tony saw the splash as the dockhand let the hawser go. He waited an instant to let Jimbo winch it well clear of the propellers then rang up 'half ahead both.'

The engine's rumble deepened further as slowly, inexorably Seaswirl gathered way. The gap between her and the land widened until it was too far for a man to jump.

With Tiger as the most experienced deckhand at the wheel Tony, as pilot, concentrated on navigating the ship towards the harbour entrance and watching out for pleasure boats which, as usual, displayed scant knowledge of the rules of the road.

Tony, gazing at them, envied their pleasure in the bright sunshine. To them the sea was a playground for a day after which they would return to their wives and lovers. Hell, their wives and lovers were probably on board with them. He stared at the small yachts racing for a buoy clustered like moths around a light, all trying to get closer at once; at the large keelers ignoring the chop and all around them, secure in their superior rights as rulers of the road, and at launches of all sizes built solely for jaunts. On one called the Gin Palace a party was going on, definitely not wives but maybe lovers scantily clad in prominence. There were speedboats with water-skiers in tow and little open boats with stoical occupants fishing.

After a while Jimbo joined him on the bridge.

"All stowed away?" asked Tony.

"Yeah, Skip".

"Any bad eggs among the new lot?"

"Nah, they're a good bunch I reckon," replied Jimbo. "Tiger here on the helm you know; he's sailed with us before. Junior might need watching, this is his first voyage. Billy and Samson could be trouble together, a couple of smart arse know-alls, but we'll see. Woody and Cooky's assistants seem OK."

"Usual bunch, then."

Jimbo only laughed by way of reply.

"Look at those plonkers dead ahead," Tony said. "Don't they know it's stupid and dangerous to anchor right in the middle of the channel? Cut in as close as you can, Tiger, and give them a blast on the siren as we go past."

"Well, would you believe it," exclaimed Jimbo, "they're waving to us. They think we're being friendly."

Seaswirl rounded the last buoy and met the long swells of the open ocean. Jimbo took over the helm and told Tiger to go down and join the others for lunch. Tony eased himself into the captain's chair placed to give him a good all-round view yet close enough to enable him to speak directly to the helmsman. He looked back along the length of the ship, now slowly rising and falling with the swell, occasionally kicking up a shower of spray creating the flicker of a rainbow in the afternoon sun.

He gazed at the receding land and asked, "How does Sal cope with this, Jimbo?"

"With what, Skip?"

"You know; this coming and going, never home for the kid's birthdays, school things, your wedding anniversaries. All those important things."

"Oh, that. She's never known anything else. Ever since we've been married that's how it's been. If she doesn't mind I don't mind. Anyway, we know it won't be forever. The money's too good to pass up at the moment, but one day when we've saved enough we'll get a little farm and grow crops."

"She doesn't worry about you not coming back?"

"Course she does, that's why she never sees me off, she can't bear it. But you bet she'll be there when we come back, just like all the other blokes' women will be."

Tony turned away and let the silence extend. He thought back to the time before he was married, when he was courting Diana. They had often gone out as a happy foursome. Jimbo and Sally already parents of two kids and seemingly content in their roles. He could see them all laughing together, enjoying each other as friends do. He could see Diana, beautiful in her skimpy black dress, dancing in the arms of a shadowy man that in his fantasy wasn't him.

Rob's call jerked him back to reality.

"Message from head office, Skipper, new fishing co-ordinates. Looks like we'll be away a bit longer than we thought. The greedy bastards want us to catch every last fish in the ocean I reckon."

Jimbo groaned. Tony only sighed; it was all the same to him, but he knew the crew wouldn't like it. This happened too often; but what the company wanted the company got. That's how it was and the crew would grumble but they would have to lump it.

♦

By the evening of their third day at sea Seaswirl was nearing the new co-ordinates where the company had calculated were their likeliest chances of success. The big trawler was hove-to riding the long swells, lights ablaze, bow pointed up into the wind as Jimbo directed the crew, about to launch the nets for the first cast.

Then Rob came into the wheelhouse, unusually excited.

"Skipper," he said. "I'm picking up a faint mayday on channel 16. Sounds like a yacht in trouble. I've got a rough bearing on it but I'll need them to transmit again so I can get a better fix."

"OK, Rob, do that. Listen out for anyone else responding. You know what the company's like; they'll want my head if we don't keep fishing. Maybe someone else closer has picked up the mayday."

Tony reached for the mike and called to Jimbo and the net crew.

"Hold the cast, Jimbo. We might have a problem. Secure the nets and the boys can take ten. You better come up to the bridge."

Jimbo burst through the bridge door just as Rob reappeared from the radio room.

"Got a good fix, Skipper. No one else is responding but I've got voice contact with the mayday vessel. Apparently they are a yacht with two badly burned people on board as a result of an electrical fire. They're down to one battery and all their solar panels are burnt so they can't recharge. They are transmitting on VHF only, which is why they are faint and probably why no one else has picked them up. They haven't given me a co-ordinate, but maybe they aren't too far away."

"Good work, Rob. Keep listening. See if you can raise them again before their batteries run right out. Also raise shipping control in Wellington and check if there are any other vessels nearer than us. And you'd better let the company know what's going on."

"Righto, Skipper."

Tony turned to Jimbo.

"Did you get all that, Jimbo? We might not be fishing for a few days yet."

"The company is not going to be impressed, Tony. You know what they're like."

"Yeah, and they know the code of the sea as well as we do; lives come first. We'll give Rob a few more minutes in case Wellington comes back with a closer vessel. If not we'll secure for fast running and head down the last radio bearing Rob got and hope we find them."

Rob poked his head back round the radio room door.

"No luck, Skipper. Their transmission faded before they could tell me a co-ordinate, but the radio direction finder bearing isn't too bad. Wellington has come back with a negative on any closer vessels and they say all air force ocean search aircraft are committed already, especially as the weather outlook is about as bad as it could be. I won't tell you what head office said, you'll only blow a fuse."

Tony laughed peremptorily and said, "Looks like we're going fishing for sailors not fish, Rob. Set the radar for extreme range and we'll track down your bearing and maybe we'll pick something up. Jimbo, would you fully secure all the gear on the fishing deck? Oh, and tell the crew what's going on; after all, it'll be their bonuses up the spout as well. I'll have a word with Woody and Cooky; none of us are going to get much sleep tonight."

The ship had already turned east south east, even further away from land, on the last known bearing, with no idea how far to run and now factoring in wind and tide to make best estimates of where the stricken yacht and dying occupants could be. The radar antennae revolved, sending its invisible rays probing out into the darkness.

The sea state was steadily worsening. Seaswirl, at full speed, began to crash and bash her way into the seas as they rose against her.

Rob came onto the bridge lit now only by the dim red night lights of the compass and data loggers.

"Wellington has come back with a possible on the name of the mayday vessel. It could be Valkyrie. Apparently she has missed their radio schedule for the last four days and no other vessel has been reported missing so it must be her. She's registered in Bermuda under the name of van Hereden. You know, that computer guy; supposed to be one of the richest men in the world."

"Never heard of him," said Tony.

"Me neither," agreed Jimbo.

"Be that as it may, Rob," continued Tony, "We'd better man the radio and the radar round the clock instead of relying on the alarms. Get one of the deckhands to spell you for a while. Jimbo, rather than normal watches we'll take it in turns. The young guys can helm for a while and Woody better have some extra help too."

By midnight the radio had been ominously silent for four hours and only the never-ending echo from the wave tops showed on the radar. Tony rang down for reduced speed as the sea pounding on Seaswirl rose to dangerous levels. Later, just before dawn, Jimbo appeared on the bridge with a tray of steaming coffee and plates of bacon and eggs, hash browns and tomatoes.

"Cooky's compliments, Skipper. Hope you don't mind if I join you?"

"Not a bit, Jimbo. You know, this reminds me of old times before we got trapped by all that company bullshit, when we could make our own decisions without worrying about the desk sailors in head office. Hell, we didn't even have a head office."

Jimbo laughed.

"Those were great days sure enough, Tony. Only thing was we couldn't catch enough to make a living with our small boat."

"Yeah, you're right. I suppose we have to be grateful the company took us on when it did, you being married and me just about to."

By tacit consent they had never spoken about Diana and the divorce, but now Jimbo decided to risk it.

"You have to admit though, Tony, you had to go and woo and win a very expensive lady to keep."

Tony replied by way of a rueful shrug, thereby ending the conversation, but he couldn't help thinking about his expensive lady. He thought how she liked to go to swanky restaurants and clubs, dressed in swanky clothes. He remembered the expensive jewellery he bought her, the top perfumes, the sports car to drive around in while he was at sea. He recalled a newspaper picture of her taken at the races accompanied by a shadowy man in a top hat who in his fantasy wasn't him.

But he didn't regret denying her nothing.

◆

By the middle of the next day they had not found Valkyrie. Tony and Jimbo pored over drift and tide tables, studied the charts and recalculated wind, tide and current effects aware that every minute counted. All of the crew searched the horizon as best they could, perched in vantage points around the ship out of the blast of the weather.

Rob relayed the disapproving calls from head office asking when they expected to resume trawling. Wellington Maritime Search and Rescue made anxious requests for information on progress and eventually confirmed the identity of the mayday vessel. At least they now knew what they were looking for, although the wind driven spume and breaking crests on top of the steep swell made seeing anything a long shot. The radar was the only real hope, but the clutter on the screen from the sea state made it hard even for that.

Tony knew that their chances of achieving a rescue would diminish rapidly if they didn't find the yacht by nightfall. The forecast was for worsening to severe gale and soon, if that eventuated, he would have to look to the safety of his own vessel. Even though Seaswirl was built to withstand the worst possible conditions the loneliest ocean in the world could throw at her she might have to hove to and ride out the storm. Then searching for a stricken vessel while being blown ever further out into the reaches of the southern ocean would have to wait.

The storm brought darkness early. Tony, Jimbo, and Woody picked away at their meal. Tony broke the silence.

"We must have missed them. They can't have drifted this far. We've been steaming at fifteen knots for thirty hours now. Their VHF would only have a range of twenty or thirty miles. Even with the drift and this wind we should have seen them hours ago."

"Provided we're tracking down the right bearing, of course," said Jimbo.

"Well, there is that. But Rob couldn't get it that wrong, could he?" asked Woody.

"Nah, he couldn't, not Rob," said Jimbo. "And you're right, Tony, we must have missed them. Mind you, in this sea that wouldn't be hard and the radar could easily miss them too. Seaswirl would have to be on top of a swell at the same time as Valkyrie to pick up an echo. Their EPIRB must have got damaged somehow as well."

They were morosely lingering over their coffees when the dining room door crashed open and Samson burst in.

"Rob's got an echo on the radar, Skipper. Can you come up at once?"

They tumbled out of their chairs and rushed up the companionway to the bridge and crowded around Rob at the glowing, flickering, green screen.

"Give it a minute, Skipper; I'm getting an echo every now and again. Must be when both vessels are at the top of a swell simultaneously and the radar has to be sweeping that bearing as well. No wonder I missed it!"

"There, I see it!" Tony shouted. "Crikey, we're about thirty miles past them. Another few minutes and we would've been out of range."

Tony turned to Woody and asked him to get back down to the engine room and stand by for some rapid alterations in engine revolutions and to make sure everyone was hanging on. They were going to turn downwind as soon as a suitable set of waves appeared and hoped they could complete the turn before a beam sea rolled Seaswirl over. Running down wind with a following sea would take all Tony's and the helmsman's skill to avoid broaching.

Once Seaswirl had made the turn Tony rang down for 'half ahead both.' He would let the giant swells roll under the vessel and risk the occasional rogue wave breaking over the stern. By going slower than the moving mountains of water he lessened the chance of Seaswirl surfing down the other side and burying her bow deep enough that she would never come up.

Rob counted down off the radar the closing range to Valkyrie. Tony had Samson up on the searchlight platform sweeping ahead in case a life raft was in the water, or something else that wouldn't show on the radar. No one gave voice to the possibility that the something else might be a body.

Even with the radar telling them Seaswirl was about half a mile away from Valkyrie, visibility was so restricted that Samson, on the big searchlight aft of the bridge, didn't pick up and illuminate the yacht until just before dawn. It had taken all of six hours to travel thirty miles. In the half light as they drew closer they could see Valkyrie was a mess; mast broken with halyards tangled, self-steering gear hanging lopsided over the stern, wheelhouse staved in. She must have been taking on seawater because she rose only sluggishly to each passing swell and sometimes was completely underwater as a crest broke over her.

Tony and Jimbo conferred.

"What do you reckon, Jimbo?"

Jimbo didn't lower his binoculars as he replied.

"Well, she's a mess all right, but somebody on board knows or knew what they're doing. There's a sea anchor out holding her bow into the wind. If there wasn't she'd be on the bottom by now. As it is she won't be afloat much longer."

"No sign of life though," observed Tony. "Probably don't even know we're here, that's if there's anybody alive on board."

"How are you going to handle this, Skipper?"

"I'll go past them, sound the siren, see if we get a reaction, then turn downwind of them. If we come up into the wind and heave to upwind of them we might be able to shelter them a bit and do something from there."

"Better not go too close. Seaswirl would smash them to bits in an instant in these seas."

"You're right, Jimbo. Someone is going to have to drift down to them in our life raft. We can pay out a rope as they go."

"I'll go, Skip. I'm qualified as a first aid officer."

"No, you won't, mate, I'll go. I'm as up with first aid as you, and you've got a wife and kids to think of. None of the others are as experienced in first aid as I am and they've all got other people to think about. If I don't make it, you are as good a skipper as me. Just promise me you won't take any risks and get home safely."

The siren got no response and, the turn across wind successfully achieved, Seaswirl drew ahead of the wallowing yacht. By juggling propeller revolutions Tony soon had her keeping a constant distance so that both vessels drifted head to wind with the storm.

Tony left Jimbo on the bridge and prepared to make the crossing clad in a wet suit and inflatable life jacket while Tiger and Samson readied the life raft and tied the lifeline to it. Launching was easily accomplished; they waited until a wave came near level with the stern deck then Tony leapt with the life raft into the water.

He gasped as the icy water broke against his wet suit. He clambered into the life raft, caught by the blasting gale and already metres away from Seaswirl. Frightening enough from the sanctuary of the ship, the ferocity of the gale at sea level shocked him to the core. With the spume and foam he couldn't tell if he was afloat or underwater.

In a few minutes and sooner than he anticipated the life raft bumped into the yacht. He registered a fleeting admiration of Jimbo's seamanship in manoeuvring Seaswirl so that the life raft was right on target first time.

As he tumbled over the tangle of wire rope that was once the yacht's rigging his inflatable life jacket caught on a broken end and tore open. He swore and moved to the companionway and hung on, conscious that if he fell overboard, that was it. He forced open the companionway door expecting to be greeted by people even if they were injured. There was no one there. In the mess of the cabin, awash with surging water, there was no sign of the occupants or any clue as to what had become of them.

Tony struggled back out into the cockpit and called up Jimbo on the hand-held.

"No one here, Jimbo. They must have abandoned ship. Can't see a life raft and no lifejackets. Don't think much to their chances. Haul me back over as quick as you can."

Tony held the RT to his ear to hear over the shriek of the wind Jimbo's crackled, "OK, Skipper."

Tony clambered back into the life raft knowing the return haul would take a lot longer against the wind and waves than the downwind slide. He hung on for dear life and watched as a bigger wave than usual bore down on him like an express train. Its crest curled and broke as it reached the life raft. He willed the boys on the rope to slacken off a bit, let him go with it and ride over it. But they saw it too late and reacted a fraction after the raft capsized sending Tony into the roiling sea.

He gasped and spluttered his way to the surface and saw that the life raft was already out of reach. The wind and waves took him further away from Seaswirl by the second. He punched the release on his inflatable life jacket and the gas hissed uselessly away through the tear. With only the wetsuit for buoyancy he spent as much time underwater as above.

19

He had one last chance to reach the yacht, but with its greater windage it was drifting faster than he was. He watched with despair as it wallowed away from him. Treading water he twisted back towards Seaswirl. Every time a swell bore him up he could see her, lights shining like beacons of hope in the gloom, the searchlights flicking back and forth over the water. She was big and solid, a safe haven so close, but the gap just too far.

He knew Jimbo would be frantically trying to turn her yet again to come to his rescue. He knew the crew would be desperately searching for him. Tony also knew that while he could see his ship they would have no chance of spotting him in the foaming cauldron. Soon all he could see when a swell lifted him up was the top of Seaswirl's mast. That meant from deck and bridge level no one could possibly see him.

Tony closed his eyes and let the waves take him as he floated as best he could. The noise of the storm receded from his consciousness and a calm came over him. He became aware of a lightening as though the storm had broken and the sun was about to come out. The battering of the wind and waves on his body eased to a gentle motion as though he was swimming lazily in the pool of their cherished home in the hills.

He felt a touch on his shoulder and turned to see his adored Diana swimming languidly beside him and smiling. Her green eyes gazed deeply into his, piercing to the core of his mind. He looked at her smooth brown skin, at her legs and arms perfectly formed. Her long blonde hair undulated in the current and the diamond ring he'd put on her finger glittered in the water.

Tony realised that in his fantasy the shadowy man was him, had always been him. He reached out to Diana intent on closing the gap, to touch her again, caressing away all that had separated them.

He wanted to keep on looking at her, but the light gained in intensity until he had to close his eyes for an instant against its brightness. Then when he opened them, just as their fingers touched, the light exploded again in a brilliant burst of incandescent colour. Tony in his semi-conscious state fleetingly, calmly accepted his end had arrived, closing the gap forever.

◆

Jimbo cursed himself and the mighty forces arrayed against them as his slight mistiming meant a huge wave pushed Seaswirl's bow back up into the wind. Now he would have to wait again for another suitable set before trying to turn her. Bitterly conscious that every second meant that Tony drifted further away, he rang down to Woody 'full astern both.' Against all the rules of prudent seamanship in such extreme conditions, it was the only thing left for Jimbo to do.

As Seaswirl gathered way astern she began to ship vast amounts of seawater over her aft fishing deck. Jimbo hoped Woody had the bilge pumps going to keep up with the inflow. But now they had a chance of catching up with Tony in the water and with all available crew manning the searchlights they might be able to spot him.

Jimbo, not aware he had been holding his breath, exhaled mightily as Samson, Billy and Jim yelled almost as one, "There he is!"

With Tony found Jimbo desperately manoeuvred Seaswirl to avoid chopping him to pieces with the propellers. As much as the gale allowed him to he carefully circled the ship around the spot illuminated on the water by Samson. It took every last bit of skilled seamanship he possessed to avoid crushing the floating body while bringing Seaswirl close enough that the searchlight shone its blinding beam right on Tony's face. Now all the crew had to do was wait for the right wave and pluck him to safety.

Jimbo, watching from the bridge, realised the three lads must have hatched a plan of what to do next because before he had time to instruct them Samson was in the water tethered to a line. Within seconds the other two had hauled him gripping Tony's lifeless body over the low gunn'l of the stern fishing deck. By the time Jimbo had yelled for Rob to take over the wheel and rushed down to the deck the lads were administering full on CPR.

"Holy cow!" cried Jimbo. "You bloody beauties. He's alive."

Tony began to splutter and cough, heaving up seawater and shivering uncontrollably.

"Carry him up to his cabin, lads; we'll sort him out there."

As soon as he was sure Tony was going to be OK Jimbo left him with Cooky spooning hot soup into him. He returned to the bridge and relieved Rob on the wheel.

"We're going to turn again. We've still got a life raft to find."

"OK, Jimbo. The raft's drift direction can't be that much different from the yacht so I'll give you the course she'd be drifting on in two shakes of a lamb's tail."

"Might take a bit of catching up with in this sea though," said Jimbo. "The raft's windage will have them skidding along like a windsurfer."

♦

Jimbo stared through the spinning clearview at the heaving sea. Dog-tired like the rest of the crew but unwilling to spell himself while there was daylight, he remained on the helm. Rob was back on the radar and every now and again yelled out a 'possible.' Their spirits sagged a little as each time it turned out to be a false echo from a particularly large wave.

Jimbo was aware that by tracking downwind they were staying with the weather front rather than letting it pass them by. Soon after four o'clock daylight began to wane and Rob had been quiet for some time. Jimbo decided to stand down the lookouts. He phoned up Woody to see if one of his lads was fresh enough to come up and give Rob a spell. A couple of hours would do them all good, then Samson or one of the others could relieve him on the wheel.

When the crew had been fed, rotating through the dining room, Cooky appeared on the bridge with a tray laden with plates of sausages and mash, bread pudding and custard, fruit and a thermos of coffee.

"Here you go, Skipper," he said. "I'll take the wheel while you tuck in if you like."

"You must be the good fairy queen," Jimbo laughed.

Cooky laughed with him before a look of intense seriousness blanked out his face as he concentrated on keeping Seaswirl's course. Jimbo surreptitiously watched him steer while he downed his food. As soon as he saw Cooky had the swing of it his thoughts turned to Tony.

"You OK here for half an hour, Cooky?" Jimbo implied with his tone that he assumed Cooky was. "Think I'll go down and check on how Tony's doing."

Jimbo knocked softly on Tony's cabin door and was relieved and surprised to hear a robust, "Enter."

Jimbo decided to dispense with pleasantries.

"Bloody glad you insisted on the crew having at least some idea how to do each other's jobs as well as their own."

"Oh yeah, why's that?" Tony was equally nonchalant.

"Cooky's on the helm, Samson's on the radar, god knows who Woody's got on the engines, I'm in here wasting time chewing the fat with you and you're lounging about in your bunk when you're supposed to be the skipper!"

Tony laughed. "Now you know what being a skipper is really like. I expect you'll be wanting my job permanently next."

"Fat chance. Anyway you look as though you're about ready to rejoin the land of the living."

"Society of seafarers, you mean. Yeah, I'm about ready to lend a hand. Tell you what, though, this little episode has given me a chance to think things through that I should have sorted out long ago."

"Like what?"

"Like getting back with Diana. Time to let go of that unrealistic fantasy. I could have sworn I was a goner when a sort of bright

23

flash somehow in that instant made me realise what an idiot I've been."

"Probably the searchlight we had fair and square on your ugly mug," laughed Jimbo.

"Yeah, well, whatever. You blokes have given me another chance at real life and I'm not going to waste it." The levity had gone from Tony's voice. "I owe you a lot, Jimbo. Not just my life but for putting up with my moods since me and Diana split."

"That's what friends are for, mate. Be nice to have you back with us all the same."

"Enough of that." Tony grinned. "No need to go all gooey on me. On to serious stuff. What's the score on the life raft?"

◆

At almost midnight Rob, back on the radar, called out to Tiger who was now on the helm.

"Better rouse the skipper. I've got a definite. They must have a reflector up."

"Which skipper?" retorted Tiger.

"Better make it both, I guess."

Jimbo came up to the bridge within minutes of getting the call and not far behind him, still a little slow, came Tony.

"Welcome back, Skipper," said Jimbo. He spoke for them all by way of deliberately handing back authority to his friend.

"Thanks, guys," said Tony as he eased himself into the captain's seat. "Let's track these souls down and get them aboard as soon as we can."

"OK, Skip. Same routine as before?"

"Yes and let's hope this time we've got some live bodies so no one has to go for a swim."

Dawn was almost upon them and a streak of clear sky on the upwind horizon hinted a possibility of the storm easing. Tony on the helm had Seaswirl stern on to the life raft. This time he wasn't so worried about taking Seaswirl close to his target. He was relieved to see that the survivors had managed to secure the line tossed them by Samson. Tiger and the other crew were rapidly hauling the raft up under the lee of the fishing deck.

In the glare of the searchlights he waited for Jimbo's signal before ringing down 'stop both' allowing the wave rolling under the big trawler to pass and then as she dipped her stern Jimbo and the crew hauled like crazy and the life raft and all in her floated aboard as though by magic.

Tony couldn't resist it. He grabbed the mike and roared over the ships loudspeakers, 'YOU BLOODY BEAUTIES.'

A couple of the crew waved that they'd heard before quickly returning to attending the survivors, rushing them forward and below to the safety of the ship's superstructure.

"Give me a course for home, Rob," called Tony as he spun the wheel to bring Seaswirl's head north west and rang down for 'full ahead both.'

The big trawler rumbled and surged to meet the swells full on as though relieved to be unshackled from the constraints of running carefully downwind.

In a few minutes Jimbo came up to the bridge.

"Six people, two badly burned and the rest OK, Skip," he reported. "Mr van Hereden is not injured and he says the six were all the people on board."

"OK, thanks Jimbo. Has he said what happened?"

"Only repeating what we picked up on the radio. Some sort of electrical fire in the galley, which explains how the two got burned. In the ensuing panic they lost control of the vessel and broached. The mast came down and holed the hull. They deployed a sea anchor but thought she was about to sink immediately and what with the fire they took their only option."

"I guess the owner's surprised we found his vessel still afloat; not that she probably still is?"

"Just grateful to be alive I think. You'll want to come and check there's nothing more we can do for the injured."

"Yeah, sure. We'll make contact with Wellington when we get closer to see if they want to do an air medi-evac. In the meantime that's the end of fishing this trip and we might as well return to normal watch keeping."

◆

Two days out from home, with the storm centre left far to the south the two skippers lounging on the bridge were speculating on the reception they were likely to get from management, when Rob called out. "Wellington says no to air evac. They say it seems we've done a good job and the risks in lifting them off are too high."

"OK, Rob," acknowledged Tony. "I'll go and have a chat with our guests, give them the good news. I think they're actually enjoying the trip. Mr van Hereden doesn't seem too upset at the loss of his yacht."

"He seems like a decent sort of bloke considering how rich he is," offered Jimbo. "Easy enough to talk to anyway."

"Quite a bit of radio chat about him and our rescue," piped up Rob. "We might be famous in our own lunchtime."

Tony and Jimbo laughed in unison.

"Yeah, right," Tony said as he left the bridge.

◆

Rob called round the wheelhouse door.

"Harbour-Master says ocean terminal berth, Skipper, not our usual number four berth."

"Righto, Rob. Wonder what's up?"

"Dunno, Skip, but it might have something to do with all these bloody helicopters buzzing around us."

Jimbo appeared on the bridge.

"All set for entering harbour, Skipper. Better get Tiger on the wheel? And Mr van Hereden wants to know if he can join us up here as we enter harbour?"

"Yes to both those, Jimbo."

Seaswirl rounded the first buoy that marked the entrance to the harbour. As the ocean swells melted away she cut through the still water as smoothly as if she had been on rails. Tony couldn't help but marvel at the contrast between the maelstrom they had recently survived and the benign beauty of their home port.

Jimbo interrupted his reverie.

"Jeepers, Skip, look at all those boats. They're heading straight for us!"

"Sound the siren, Tiger," ordered Tony. "Make the silly buggers give us room."

"You've got to laugh, Skip; they really are waving this time," said Jimbo. "It's some sort of welcoming flotilla. We better be friendly seeing we've got the VIP on board."

As Seaswirl neared the ocean terminal berth normally reserved for cruise ships Mr van Hereden came up to the bridge and gazed at the harbour around him.

"I owe you and your crew a great deal, Tony. It might be about to get a lot busier then you two realise." He included Jimbo in his gaze and gestured towards the media helicopters and flotilla. "So I want to express my sincere gratitude to you both now while I've got the chance and offer you my help in any way possible should you need it in the future for anything whatsoever."

Tony caught Tiger's eye and then stared at Jimbo, willing them to mind their manners and not mention the crews' lost bonuses. To his relief Jimbo only shrugged and said, "Glad we could help."

"Looks like we've got a reception committee dockside. No wonder they wanted us to tie up at ocean terminal," observed Tony. "Jimbo, there's Sal with your kids."

"Crikey, I'd better go and get the mooring party spruced up and myself too with this audience."

Jimbo left the wheelhouse.

Tony rang down for Woody to slow the engines to minimum revolutions and Seaswirl glided abreast of her designated berth. He watched Jimbo on the foc'sle give Samson the nod to heave the mooring line to the dockhand waiting on shore. As Jimbo paid out the hawser Tony rang 'half astern both' to check the ship's forward way and then after a pause rang 'all stop.'

As soon as he heard Jimbo call over the hand-held that the stern line was fast he said to Tiger, "Right rudder," and Seaswirl slowly inched, beam on, towards her berth. The gap closed until there was none at all.

Jimbo's voice crackled over the bridge speaker.

"All secure, Skipper."

Tony rang down to Woody for the last time, 'finished with engines.' And as the rumble of the engines, the ever-present symphony to any voyage, died away to a profound silence Mr van Hereden said to Tony, "That was the classiest bit of ship handling I've ever had the privilege to see."

Tony, totally concentrated on manoeuvring his ship safely alongside was startled to find Mr van Hereden still on the bridge. He smiled briefly.

"All part of the service."

The lowering of the gangway re-establishing Seaswirl's connection with land served as a signal for company men in suits and city officials sporting chains of office to come charging on board. With a quick 'well done Tony,' the suits whisked Mr van Hereden away to the civic reception waiting on the wharf.

Tony turned to Jimbo and the rest of the watching crew and said, "No civic reception for us, guys, but go and enjoy the real reception I know you're waiting for from your loved ones. I can see they're all there on the wharf."

Tony followed slowly behind his crew, smiling not a little enviously, as they made human reconnection each in their own way. He stood behind his crew and their families, wives, girlfriends, mothers, fathers and uncles as they watched the dignitaries trying to outdo each other with obsequious speeches towards Mr van Hereden while the media jockeyed for position. Tiring of the spectacle, the crew turned away as one, ready to depart and scatter until the next voyage.

On the point of following them Tony heard his name called and turned back to see Mr van Hereden shouldering his way through the throng trailed by a couple of anxious company men and behind them someone else who, in the brilliant sun and shadowy confusion, he couldn't make out.

"Tiresome all this, don't you find?" Mr van Hereden enquired as he caught up with him, as though Tony was a frequent beneficiary of civic receptions.

Before a surprised Tony could reply Mr van Hereden said, "Before you go there's someone I'd like you to meet." He turned and gestured for the company suits to step aside and said, "This is my daughter, though she's much more than my daughter is Anna. She pretty well runs the whole show now and a fine job she makes of it too."

Tony registered nothing except 'daughter' and 'Anna.' Although she wasn't beautiful in the sense that his wife had been he could see that this person, Anna, had something about her that struck him as - yes, 'striking' was the word he thought. Tall and slim with auburn hair, and strikingly attractive.

She put out her hand to shake his and as Tony touched her fingers a flash of light blinded him. As he closed his eyes he was taken back to when the vision of Diana came to him as he almost drowned and for an instant he was drowning again. But then he felt the firm hand grip his own and opened his eyes to see Anna, still holding his hand, gazing at him with a wry smile.

"Your ship is trying to tell you something, I think. She blinded you with a reflection of the sun on the wheelhouse window as she moved with the tide." Anna laughed. "She doesn't like you talking to another woman."

Tony laughed with her and held on to her hand. She made no effort to relax her grip. She returned his intent look with an openness that took his breath away. He knew then that some sort of chasm had been crossed, a precious connection made.

A gap filled. A gap closed.

◆　◆　◆

The Netherton Knicker Nicker

Constable Kevin Taylor fingered the official-looking letter and pondered its contents. For weeks the constable had been faxing nil crime reports to regional headquarters. Nil crimes committed, nil suspects interviewed, nil persons helping police with enquiries and nil arrests. No one detained and zero complaints.

There wasn't space on the report for the things he actually did; such as clipping young Jimmy Shaw around the ear for shoplifting a choc bar from Nanjit Singh's Four Square; taking the car keys off Bill Watson every Saturday night *before* he left the bar, or banging the heads together of the rowdies that started a fight in the rugby club last Thursday night.

All good old-fashioned small town Kiwi policing.

Not to mention the wandering stock returned to the rightful owners or the emergency dash taking the chainsaw casualty; the kicked by horse, cow or bull; the concussed, injured, cut and scraped into the base hospital in Thames.

The constable leaned back in the police issue chair and read the letter again. Emblazoned with the seal of the District Commissioner of Police, Central Division, it made official what had been threatened for some time. The constable sighed, levered his considerable bulk out of the chair and left the small annex that served as Netherton's police station.

One short hallway and he was in the kitchen of the police house that had been his and Grace's home for the last twelve years. He showed Grace the letter.

"It's official, they're going to close us down."

"At last, thank goodness," said Grace. "We can escape this boring little place and live a little."

"They call it rationalisation. Because there's no crime to speak of they think no police presence is needed. Don't they realise that there is no crime because I'm here keeping a lid on it?"

Kevin stomped around the kitchen waving the letter.

"They're going to post me to the city; say my experience will be invaluable. They must be mad; I haven't served on a city beat for nearly twenty years. I like it here."

"Super! The city! I'll be able to see more of my mum, go shopping while you're working, catch up on movies. It'll be nice to be near a decent library again." Grace looked imploringly at Kevin. "You know how lonely I get here."

"You haven't been listening. I don't want to go. I want to see out my service here. The city is for go-getting hotshots, not run-down old coppers like me."

"I don't care. You're always off with that ridiculous 'council', drinking and goodness knows what when you're not working. It's time we... I left this backwater."

Kevin looked sadly at the stranger that was Grace his wife of two and a half decades and fleetingly wondered where she had gone. He said quietly, "I'm going out on patrol."

"On patrol! Straight down the pub I'll bet," Grace called after him as he softly closed the door.

He *was* heading for the pub, but Grace's jibe made him pause. He turned away from the direction of the pub and instead walked in the gathering dusk along the main street towards the rugby grounds on the edge of town.

♦

The constable sat on a plank that served as a seat and gazed at the setting sun framed by the goal-posts and marvelled at the rosy tint that disguised the ordinariness. He couldn't leave this place or these people. Apart from a few ratbags who shop-lifted or were articulate only with their fists, there was little to disturb the peace. His kind of policing soon had them on the straight and narrow without a conviction against their name. He wondered whether he should have been more modern and done everything by the book, reported everything, arrested everyone who so much as swore in public.

31

The constable sighed for the second time that evening; told himself to snap out of it and get on with a bit of police work, his style.

He smiled to himself as he saw Billy Watson's car parked outside the police station, a sure sign Billy was already across the road, glass in hand. The constable checked the police letterbox as he walked back past and pocketed Billy's car keys. He saw Grace moving about inside, telly flickering, but he didn't go in.

◆

Constable Kevin shouldered open the pub door to the familiar heavy smell of hops, the clink of glasses and the buzz of conviviality that passed for Saturday night in Netherton. He acknowledged with a smile and a wave the shouts and g'days and the inevitable, from some clever dick, "Watch out! The law's arrived."

Except for a couple of scruffy teenagers sitting at a corner table he knew everyone in the bar. He made a mental note to keep an eye on the teenagers; if they looked like getting drunk he would put the wind up them and threaten to book them for underage drinking.

He made his way through the throng, having a word here and there as he went, acknowledging Billy Watson's 'Cheers.' Eventually he landed at the tall table where his friends, jocularly known as 'the town council' and the table as 'the chambers,' were leaning. As usual there was Joe Smith, captain of the rugby club and owner of the local trucking business; Andy Wilson, stock agent; Larry James, vet; and Tom Clark, garage proprietor.

Joe pushed a full one over to the constable.

"You're a couple behind, Kev so you'd better get this down you."

Kev took a long pull and emptied the glass in one.

"Must be thirsty work this fighting crime, eh, Kev?" joked Andy.

"Got some bad news, boys. The powers that be are going to close down the station and ship me out so I won't be fighting crime here much longer," said Constable Kevin. "Pity there's no real crime to fight."

♦

When the malty fug in Kevin's brain cleared enough that he could ignore the street bell no longer he roused from his Sunday morning slumber.

"All right, all right,' he mumbled. "Keep your shirt on."

He stumbled through the annex and opened the street door.

"Mrs Smith! Nothing happened to Joe, I hope?"

"No, nothing like that, constable," replied Joe Smith's wife, Jean.

"What then? Can't it wait until Monday?" he said testily. "We don't normally work on Sundays."

"No, it can't wait. Some pervert has stolen my washing."

"Stolen your washing! What do you mean?"

"My underwear that I'd left on the line has disappeared."

"I don't believe anyone in Netherton would do anything like that. Must have been those two scruffy teenagers I saw in the pub last night. Give me a list of what's missing and I'll look into it, I mean, get onto it...ah...as soon as possible."

Constable Kevin carefully entered the crime in the day book, then hearing Grace in the kitchen made his way there.

"First crime of the week, Gracie. First of the month actually. At last something to report," he crowed. "Some pervert stole Joe Smith's missus's underwear."

"Pervert!" snorted Grace. "They'd have to be desperate to steal her smalls. She's one big lady!"

"No need to be nasty. I'll get right on to the case tomorrow. Now, as soon as I've finished breakfast I'm off out fishing with the boys."

Grace called softly to his departing back, "Have a nice day."

♦

Monday morning before Constable Kevin had time to plan how he was going to catch the underwear thief, Mrs Wilson burst into the Police Station.

She spat out, "The dirty degenerate has pinched mine too."

"Calm down, Angela," soothed the constable. "Pinched your what?"

"My underwear, just like Jean Smith's."

Constable Kevin observed Angela Wilson. 'She was a bit of all right; a different kettle of fish compared to poor old Joe's missus. Angela Wilson's underwear would be worth taking. Maybe the thief wasn't such a twisted pervert after all. Still a pervert though, he mused.

"Give me the details, Angie and I'll get right on it."

The constable tactfully ignored the lady's blushes.

In truth he didn't have a clue where to start. Tom Clark, whose garage was out on the main road, had seen the scruffy teenagers leave before the latest incident. The constable had no leads but he did have another entry for the day book. Two crimes in a week. Things were looking up.

♦

After a dinner that they might each as well have eaten alone, Kevin made for the door, calling out as he went.

"Off on patrol, Grace. Don't wait up."

"Don't worry, I won't. Have one for me," Grace muttered to the empty room.

On a week night Constable Kevin wasn't surprised to see the pub half empty. He *was* surprised that Joe Smith and Andy Wilson weren't in their usual spot. Larry James and Tom Clark were the only 'council members' present.

"Where's Joe and Andy?"

"They've been and gone, mate," replied Larry. "Something about being on a promise."

"Wow, that'll be a first. For Joe anyway. Lucky old Andy," smirked the constable.

"Yeah. Apparently this panty burglar's got the wives going."

The next day Larry's wife Christine reported another theft just like the others. Constable Kevin, who had made no progress on the investigation, asked in exasperation, "Why do you ladies leave your smalls out on the washing line overnight?"

"We don't want you men in this dump seeing our frillies," replied Christine. "It's embarrassing."

"Well, some bloke is seeing plenty of them and the longer it goes on without me catching him the more it *embarrasses* me."

The next night in the pub the husbands of all three victims, Joe, Andy and Larry, only made a cursory appearance, saying they had things to attend to at home.

"Nudge, nudge, wink, wink, you know what I mean," they chorused.

"Just you and me now then, Tom," said Kevin. "How about we stake out your place tonight? See if we can catch the bugger in the act."

"Crikey! All right then, Kev. If you don't catch him soon this pub will go broke. Then where would we go for a drink?"

"Get your missus to hang up something suitable and I'll come around at midnight."

Tom and the constable spent the night peering out the Clarks' kitchen window hoping for a glimpse of the nocturnal panty purloiner. At dawn they called it quits; although neither could be certain that nothing had happened during the considerable times when the beer and whisky chasers induced slumber.

♦

The constable faxed off his weekly report prominent with details of three major crimes and the measures he had taken to solve them, including all night surveillance which meant extra overtime. Maybe the brass wouldn't be so hasty in shutting Netherton down now. What a stroke of luck ...

His reverie was interrupted by the street door crashing open. Toni, Tom Clark's wife reported breathlessly, "The dirty bas... pervert's taken my best lingerie. I was getting it all nice for our wedding anniversary. It's our thirtieth on Friday you know."

"What! How can that be? Asked Constable Kevin. "Tom and I kept our eyes peeled all night and we didn't see a thing."

"From the number of empties I've cleared away this morning I doubt you kept your eyes peeled *all* the time," retorted Mrs Clark scornfully.

"Well, I'll get right on to it Toni, don't you worry. I'll catch him sooner or later."

◆

The constable didn't have to shoulder his way into the bar that evening. It was practically empty. There was no one at 'the chambers' for the first time ever as far as he could recall. So he leaned on the bar instead and said to Jim Mathews, the rheumy old publican, "Where is everybody?"

"G'day, Kev. The rumour is that this panty pervert has got all the ladies revved up," wheezed old Jim. "Bit of excitement. The blokes are getting a bit of 'how's your father' for the first time in living memory. I'm thinking of hanging some of my old duck's thingies out myself. Maybe my luck will change."

"Well, I never. Whatever next or rather who's next?"

"Speaking of who's next; has your missus had anything pinched yet?"

"I dunno, haven't asked her and she hasn't said."

"Nobody, not even a sex maniac pervert would pinch stuff off a cop's wife. Here," cackled Jim, "have one on the house, build up your strength for your relentless fight against crime."

"Cheers, mate."

Kevin raised his glass, unconcerned as always about drinking on duty.

◆

The next few weeks Constable Kevin's fax reports contained details of the continued thefts from clotheslines of women's underwear. Some from the same clotheslines. The rumour mill running hot in the pub and rugby club was that some of the wives and even the husbands were pegging up underwear in the hopes their turn would come.

The constable questioned Nanjit Singh in the back storeroom of his Four Square shop.

"You're sure you're not out pinching petticoats, Nanjit? You seem to have a few boxes of the stuff here."

"No way, Constable Kev! This all very new stock, very big demand. This is a convenience store, you see, just like silly TV advertisement says."

Somehow Nanjit managed to nod and shake his head simultaneously. Constable Kev caught himself nodding along with the shopkeeper.

"Well, if you hear any gossip when the ladies come in let me know."

"OK, Constable Kev, will do straight away, no mucking about! Here take this very latest fashion very popular negligee for your lovely Grace, free of charge."

The Constable glared at Nanjit for a moment to see if he was taking the micky. Seeing nothing there but radiant honesty said, "Thanks Nanjit, I will take the negligee but I can't take it for free."

"OK, Constable Kev, whatever you say," said Nanjit, his head wobbling fit to fall off. "Still very cheap. I think your lovely Grace will like very much so."

◆

The constable presented the gift to Grace that evening when he got home.

"Um, ah ..." He fumbled for the right words. "Got something for you."

"Don't tell me you've come over all shy after all these years, Kev?" she taunted. "Come on, show me what you've got."

Kev unwrapped the parcel for her.

"Why, you old dog, you. I do believe you're blushing. Come here. I've got something for you too."

With that she planted a kiss fair and square.

◆

The following morning the constable was leaning back in his familiar chair going through the mail when he spotted an envelope with the District Commissioners seal on it. He opened it and read the contents. He sighed, levered his bulk up and made his way from the annex through the hall into the kitchen.

Grace was sitting at the table and the aroma of brewing coffee drifted from the stove.

"You're just in time for coffee, dear."

Kev sat down beside her and showed her the letter.

"They're not going to shut us down after all. Seems the city press got hold of the story. They're calling it 'Netherton's Knicker Nicker' and the bad publicity must have made the Commissioner change his mind. Would you be too upset if we stayed?"

"Not if we could spend more time together, once you catch the Nicker. I've seen Joe and Jean and all the other wives and husbands spending time together for the first time in years. The town has come alive. And I can't remember when you last gave me a gift as lovely as that negligee," said Grace. "It's just like old times."

◆

The crime wave continued. The constable said to Grace, "I don't understand it. I've been trying to nail this degenerate for weeks now. It's gone way beyond a joke. I thought things might ease up now that it looks as though the station is going to stay open."

"Why would you think that, dear? I ran into Jean and Angela down at the Four Square today and they said they hope the thief never stops because they haven't had so much attention from their men in years."

"I wouldn't be surprised if those clever ladies were pinching each others or their own, for crying out loud."

The constable scratched his head.

"Gracie, next time you see them down at Nanjit's give them the word I'm on to them, will you? We can't have all these women traipsing around Netherton in the small hours. Somebody really might get hurt."

The next morning the Constable lingered in the kitchen over a hot coffee. Gracie thumped the basket of dry washing on the table.

"The Knicker Nicker has struck again. The negligee you bought me has gone."

"No kidding," said Kevin. "He took his time getting round to you. I was beginning to wonder if you were the thief."

"Don't be silly. What would I want with a lot of ladies underwear?" retorted Grace. "I do know how the others feel now though; really, it's quite exciting."

◆

The constable rolled over, lightly caressed Grace's shoulder and kissed her softly before whispering, "Accident down at the main road. Back soon."

Accustomed to emergencies at all hours she barely stirred apart from fleetingly grasping his hand, just as she used to, as though imploring him not to go but knowing he must.

He crept out into the dark night. He drove the ute towards the main road, just in case, before circling back to the rugby grounds where there was a large drum incinerator round the back of the clubhouse, well out of sight. He stood looking a little guiltily at the boxfuls of underwear, got a fire going and ruefully ran the soft silk and lace of Grace's new negligee through his rough fingers before, smiling sadly to himself, he tossed it into the incinerator.

Soon he warmed to the task and in went the bras, the knickers, the petticoats and some things he couldn't identify.

In the pre-dawn blackness someone coughed. The constable started.

"Christ almighty! I didn't notice you lot creep up. You buggers nearly gave me a heart attack. What are you blokes doing here at this hour of the morning?"

"I was up checking our backyard." Joe answered for all of them. "Thought I heard the Knicker Nicker prowling about. Saw your ute go by with no lights on. Thought you might be on the Nicker's case so I celled the 'councillors' in case you needed a hand."

Andy, Tom, Larry and even old Jim and Nanjit stood silently by, Nanjit nodding in agreement as usual.

"So what are you burning at four o'clock in the morning?" asked Joe. "As if we didn't know."

"Well, now you do know! So what?" Kev challenged.

"So we'll give you a hand to get rid of the evidence. Come on, boys."

Each man grabbed items and tossed them in the incinerator.

"Suppose this means the end of the crime wave eh, Kev? Pity if it is because we reckon it was the best thing that ever happened to Netherton."

"That may well be, boys, but the whole thing was getting out of hand. It wasn't just me towards the end," protested the constable. "You blokes or your wives were pinching each other's stuff, for goodness sake!"

He tossed another frilly on the fire.

"Anyway the brass would have smelled a rat sooner or later and sent some hotshot city detective down here then we would all have been in trouble. Hotshot detectives don't have much sense of humour, you know."

"Yeah," old Jim grumbled, "but my pub's going broke since you blokes are always at home with your wives now."

"Nah, you won't go broke," said Kev. "I'm going to reconvene the 'council' only this time Gracie's coming too."

"Jean too," said Joe Smith

"Same for Angela," said Andy Wilson.

"That goes for Chrissy," said Larry James.

"Toni would be a starter," said Tom Clark.

"That's settled then," said Constable Kev. "How about we keep this little episode to ourselves, guys? If things get a bit quiet again in future just give me the nod and maybe the knicker bandit will strike again."

They all laughed and slapped Kev on the back.

"Good on you, mate."

Kev spoke up again.

"One more thing. I think it's about time Nanjit joined the 'council,'" he turned to Nanjit. "I know you're not supposed to drink alcohol, mate, but you won't be the only one on the lemonade because that's all I'm drinking from now on. Bring Mrs Singh. It's about time we gave this town a decent rev up and the ladies have sure shown us how to do that."

◆ ◆ ◆

Ageless Beauty

I liked mowing my lawns. My dear wife Angela occasionally suggested I buy a ride-on or pay someone to do it, like everyone else in our street. Even though it takes me longer and longer as the years go by, I consider pushing the mower up and down keeps me fit. Besides, the mindlessness of the task lets me think without getting maudlin, mostly about Angela and the pride she once took in our grounds.

"Robert," she used to say, "you'll do yourself an injury if you're not careful. You can't sit behind a desk all week then expect to mow an acre and a half without paying a price."

I mostly laughed at her, though touched by her concern. I mean, I think a lifetime in operating theatres and medical research labs qualified me to know best. Turned out she was the one who needed to take care.

♦

"You wouldn't think a person as famous as him would mow his own lawns would you?" said Sybil, twitching back the lace curtains to better observe the activity across the street.

"Who?"

Gerald, Sybil's husband, lowered the newspaper, which he had hoped rendered him invisible.

"Oh do keep up, Gerald. Sir Robert in number seven, of course." Sybil stamped her foot in irritation. "The poor man must be hot; I'll take him an iced tea."

"Not only famous, ancient as well, silly old git. If you're taking him refreshment ask him if he wants to come out to dinner again. Can't do my chances of getting on the council any harm to be seen looking out for a respected senior citizen."

Gerald put down his newspaper.

♦

As I mowed near the footpath edge of the front lawn I saw out of the corner of my eye that dreadful woman from across the road. She marched across with a tray of drinks. How I wished for a car to come along at that moment and bowl her over. I concentrated on keeping outwardly amiable while inwardly I groaned.

"Good morning, Bob," the woman simpered. "I could see you are working hard and you seemed to enjoy the drink I brought you last time you mowed your lawns. Gerald and I thought you might like another."

"Thank you, so thoughtful um, ah, ah ..." I'd forgotten her name so busy was I saying to myself, 'My name's Robert! I hate Bob except from my closest and dearest friends and you aren't one of them.'

"Sybil, Sybil Hinton from across the street at number two. You do remember don't you? We took you to dinner at the Ascot Room a fortnight ago."

Sybil peered at him anxiously, afraid her cultivation of Sir Robert might have been in vain.

"Of course I remember."

What else could I say knowing full well what was coming and I was trapped?

"Gerald and I are going to 'Monde Cuisine' for dinner and we'd like you to come."

Why these blasted neighbours of mine meddle in my life is beyond me. Why they insist on 'taking' me out to dinner, won't take no for an answer, irritates the bejesus out of me. 'Take' me to dinner; yeah right. I'll make a little bet with myself; I'll end up paying. They seem to think I have a hankering to go to every damn overpriced restaurant in the city before I die. Nouvelle cuisine at my age. What a farce; two scallops on a dinner plate the size of a helipad. Ask for my steak 'well done' how I like it and the bloody thing might as well still be mooing. Ah well, at least it's a night away from the pathetic sham that passes for television nowadays.

♦

"Here we are then Bob," proclaimed Gerald, as though he had accomplished a miracle by driving the short distance from their leafy suburb to the inner city.

"Drop Bob and me off right at the restaurant door, Gerald," commanded Sybil. "We don't want to tire the old gentleman out, do we? No point in us all getting wet either."

"Your wish is my command. Got to keep the weaker sex happy, eh Bob?" chortled Gerald.

"Oh, do shut up, Gerald," snapped Sybil. "Go and park the car while I get Bob inside."

The two of them carried on as though Sir Robert was invisible. He fervently wished he was.

♦

Roberto, the maitre d', recognised Sybil from a previous visit and the elderly gentleman with her was vaguely familiar. Roberto's heart sank when he saw the woman and the old boy remove their coats and shake off the rain drops all over his polished floor. Why couldn't they do that in the foyer like everybody else? However, he put on his professional face and bent slightly at the waist to give the merest suggestion of a bow.

"Good evening, madam, and welcome. Table for you and your father?"

"No, for three," Sybil snapped back, "and this isn't my father!"

"Very well, madam."

What the fuck did Roberto care if the elderly gent wasn't her father. She was fawning over him as if he were, apart from the snappy lapse from which she quickly recovered.

"This way, madam and sir. Veronica will be your waitress for the evening."

◆

Roberto, the maitre d' didn't recognise me but I did him. His name was Robert then, like mine, long before he'd elevated himself into haute cuisine. We'd had a successful encounter in the operating theatre of Middlemore where he'd been the fortunate recipient of my team's attention to his cardio-vascular system. But it didn't seem appropriate to remind him of that.

◆

Veronica eyed her new customers, thoughts rolling through her brain like a running monologue. 'This old git should be in bed, it's past his bedtime. Mine too. Christ, my feet are killing me. I hoped that no one else would come in on a night like this. My last punters, that family with the snot-nosed kids, should have been my last. I bet this lot won't leave a tip either. God, I hate this job.'

Aloud she said, "Good evening, folks. My name is Veronica and I'm thrilled to be your table executive for the evening. Will your father be requiring drinks this evening, madam?"

"Of course he will and he's not my father!"

◆

I had to laugh; but only to myself. Sybil took exception to my being taken as her father, twice in as many minutes.

I liked this restaurant the first time I came, even though the food was expensive crap. Apart from observing the successful use Roberto had unknowingly made of his extension of life, the waitress's outfits were titillating. Short black skirts that rode up their thighs when they bent over.

I didn't consider it an insult to my dear departed that I enjoyed looking at firm young bums. Indeed, I think Angela would have appreciated them too. And their loose white blouses meant I could see down their cleavage when they served at table.

I observed from their lack of modesty they thought me a sexless dried-up old codger no longer interested in their female attributes when, in fact, I was very interested. I didn't disabuse the waitresses, just helped myself to an eyeful and recalled times not so long ago when my one true love would have given any one of these hotties a run for their money.

♦

"Ordered yet, Sybil?" brayed Gerald, shrugging off his coat and showering nearby diners with raindrops. "Devil of a job finding a park. Don't know why we come here."

♦

'Spare me,' Veronica thought. 'You insist on coming here, you screaming git, because it's expensive and where all the towns' big-noters come and you will be seen doing good taking an old man to dinner.'

Veronica's smile betrayed none of her inner turmoil.

'If this lot doesn't make up their minds and order soon I'll be off to Casualty to have both feet amputated. Artificial ones might be a godsend in this prick of a job.'

She stood poised with pad and pencil at the ready.

'I'll have to watch the old boy. I'd seen him looking up Rose's skirt when she leaned over serving the next table He wasn't as docile as he looked. Gave him a thrill. As for Gormless Gerald and Strident Sybil, I've never seen a more sexless couple. He didn't even look at my tits when I dipped to pour his water. Mind you, he's got Strident's beady eyes on him.'

♦

The water glasses were way too heavy and the splayed shape made them tricky for old guys like me to hold. I let my half-full glass slip,

46

spilling water over the table to drip on the floor. Delicious Veronica hustled over and I got a good view of her jugs as she mopped up.

I was pleased to see Sybil and Gerald were steaming with embarrassment as the few remaining diners, bored with their partner's small talk, ogled the commotion.

◆

'Oh fuck,' Roberto mouthed to himself. 'What is it with these people and water? First they drip all over my floors, now they're splashing over the carpet.'

He hurried over as Veronica bent to mop the table.

'Wow! That Veronica is a piece of work. What an arse and look at that old boy ogling her knockers. Wouldn't mind getting a good look myself.'

He said aloud, "Here, let me help you clean up, Vee."

◆

Veronica looked daggers at Roberto as though telepathing her thoughts.

'If there's anything I hate its being called Vee. My name is Veronica, you sleazebag.'

Her professional smile remained fixed.

'You make us wear these ridiculous outfits so you can perve, you creep. Then wonder why the customers do the same.'

Out loud she said, "No, that's fine. I can manage."

◆

I winked at the poor waitress, sorry, table executive, to let her know I sympathised with her plight. Her eyebrows rose in surprise that I'd picked up her signals and then she winked back.

I wondered if I could ditch those two sycophants, Sybil and Gerald and maybe invite Veronica to visit me sometime. I'm sure

Angela wouldn't mind a beauty again gracing her garden and Veronica would have nothing to fear from me. After all I am eighty-one and a knight of the realm. I wondered if she was sick of her job and whether she would consider becoming my gardener. I could see her in short shorts and a tight tee-shirt dark with sweat as she pushed the old mower up and down. Now that would stick it up Gormless and Strident.

I suddenly felt much better about picking up the bill and decided that Veronica was in for a very large tip. As she helped me on with my coat, I asked, "Interested in horticulture at all?"

Her smile, anything but professional, broadened into a grin. For the first and only time that evening I'd got an honest reply and without a word spoken.

◆　◆　◆

Upmarket Skip Men

Colin, now a connoisseur of other people's dreck, had been in a previous life a trader of junk bonds. He considered that a neat irony; just a different type of junk. Although junk bond trading had got him into seriously deep trouble he now considered it kismet as his fortunes were on the up and up.

Ambrose had never managed to be successful at anything. That had changed when he met Colin over a deliciously full skip placed outside a major renovation job of an old colonial mansion in Remuera. Initial hostility borne of rivalry soon subsided as each amassed more treasures than both their ex-supermarket trolleys could contain.

"Nothing more here, mate," said Ambrose.

Colin got out the list of Waste Management customers current for that week he had obtained from the office girl by trading a make-up set with only the mascara missing.

"Looks like the next skip is just down the road. Office renovation."

Off they went, pushing their booty like a couple of burglars, living the dream, beholden to no-one but themselves. Skip-men and proud of it. Earning a living; making an almost honest buck.

Ambrose relished the sun on his back filtering through the leafy trees lining the quiet street.

"Not a bad morning's haul, Col," he said as they unloaded the trolleys into their van bodied Mercedes eight wheeler that gleamed in the sun. "Glad I met up with you, mate, otherwise I'd still be on the one skip at a time circuit."

"Nothing like bringing a bit of tee and em to the job."

Colin grunted as he hefted a three legged table that should have had four onto the hydraulic load lifter. Ambrose was quiet for a minute.

Then he said, "Ah, time and motion. Thought you meant something else, like rude."

"Not me Ambro. No time for that sort of thing now. Come on; the next skip awaits."

Ambrose, who carried a bit more weight than Colin, mostly around his midriff, was feeling the morning's exertion.

"Why again is it that we park the truck out of sight of the skips?"

"Not too sure myself, pal, but I have the feeling that the guys on the site turn a blind eye to us scavenging. They see a couple of down and out no-hopers rather than the rubbish professionals we are."

Ambrose, ever literally-minded, said, "I wouldn't say we're rubbish professionals. We do know what we're doing and we *do* actually look like down and out no-hopers."

"You know what I mean," replied Colin testily. "The site foremen don't mind no-hopers helping themselves, but they do mind professionals like us poking about. They'd want to charge us even though in my book we're helping them out."

"Yeah, the greedy bastards," Ambrose agreed morosely.

Truck locked, they set off in the other direction towards the main road where the office block reno was underway. He brightened up as he said to Colin, "Bet you never thought you'd end up pushing a supermarket trolley along the street like an old hobo."

"Don't talk about bets to me, mate. Let me tell you how I came to be in the skip contents re-cycling business, if you must know."

Colin continued speaking as they pushed their trolleys.

"I kept a picture in my wallet of the perfect hand a poker player can ever get; the Royal Flush. I never was dealt such a hand, but I lived in hope. More than that I lived in certainty one day I would strike the big payoff. I told myself then I would give up the gambling game for the mug's game it was. My ex-wife, Josephine, called it that; a mug's game."

Colin paused and, as though suddenly tired, sat down on a low scoria stone wall fronting the garden of a brick and half-timbered 1930s style two-storied house.

"Ah..." he sighed, "Josie, one of my regrets when I think about her. And the kids. Grown up now and making real lives for themselves. None of them followed me into the gambling fraternity."

Colin spoke whimsically as though pining for what might have been.

"For a while I thought Wayne, the youngest - although he would be nearly thirty now - would be my perfect offsider in the big plays. He had a terrific head for maths and a colossal memory. He could match me hand for hand in bridge and poker before he was fourteen."

"What happened; why didn't Wayne partner you?" Ambrose asked unaware that recalling the past was upsetting his friend. "You could have made a killing in the casinos?"

"Unfortunately his mother influenced him out of it. He couldn't have come into the casino until he was eighteen anyway, so maybe it was a good thing. Now he is a top man at Ace Computers, so I believe, but I haven't seen him since he married that pretty girl from down the line whose name I can't remember."

"Look, Col, sorry I brought it up. Didn't mean to drag up your painful past. How about we get along to that skip before some other no-hoper beats us to it?"

Ambrose levered himself up from the wall.

"That's all right, mate," Colin replied. "I might as well tell you the whole story now I've started. Josie was a stunner and smart to boot. We had a pretty good life. She brought up the kids while I brought home the bacon so to speak. Trading bonds is money for old rope. God knows why they pay such huge bonuses. Compensate us for putting in the boring hours I suppose. Trouble is I took my eye off the ball and, when trading bonds, that is the one thing you cannot afford to do."

The breath he took was more like a sigh.

"It all started to go pear-shaped when I had my fiftieth birthday, which coincided with thirty years of service at Kensington Investments. Don't get me wrong, I enjoyed the party in my

51

honour, unaccustomed as I was to such things. It was in the days and weeks after that that I noticed I was still dealing in low grade bonds, much as I had when I started. My colleagues with the same length of service had long since departed either out or upstairs. My immediate superiors were younger than Wayne. I know I became hard to live with."

Colin mopped his forehead. Ambrose wasn't sure whether it was the sun or the heat of recall that caused his friend to reach for his handkerchief before he continued.

"Josie, with the kids grown-up enough not to need chasing after, was savouring her freedom. She took up painting and, give her her due, got good at it quickly. Suddenly, almost overnight it seemed she was never home, always off somewhere either painting or showing. She began to do well out of it. I became a bit of a grump. Not with her, I see now, but at myself at being stuck in a hopeless rut, hating my job while she was doing something she loved. I was envious I suppose; even a little jealous. She took it personally; didn't have time for me anymore, it seemed. But I miss her still.

"I decided that at my age then I had one last chance to make it big, get the respect of my wife and kids back again. I was going to go out and clean up on the professional gambling circuit. After all, I always won the amateur whist tournaments. None of my old friends would play against me because I always won. Never mind. By then I didn't have any old friends.

"How was I to know that after a lifetime of toeing the line, playing it safe I would turn into an addict? I just loved those cards, loved the promise they held. I used to get out my picture of the Royal Flush and imagine it mine."

Ambrose looked worriedly at his friend.

"We should be moving, Col. We haven't had lunch yet and we've still got that skip to do."

But being an ex-gambler himself he was curious enough to ask, "Did you ever strike the Royal Flush?"

"Never happened. I got deep in with some heavy types in games that went higher stakes every time I lost. The suits upstairs at

Kensington found out and 'let me go' because they reckoned it wasn't a good look. My job and our house went the same way as Josie and the kids. I lost the lot."

There was silence as Colin's voice trailed away. With a sigh he stood up and said to Ambrose, "Come on, mate. The past is the past, gone now and no point crying over spilt milk and all that."

"That's about the same as my story, Col," Ambrose offered, "but I'm sure we don't want to go into that now."

He was relieved that his friend had snapped out of the reverie he himself had induced with what he saw now as insensitive probing.

"No, no, quite all right, old chap. Fire away."

Colin sat down again.

"Like you," Ambrose began hesitantly, "I couldn't help myself. My life revolved around the ponies. I studied Best Bets, the racing pages ad nauseam. I was an acknowledged expert. Ask me anything about horse racing and I could tell you who the best trainers were, which horse went best on a heavy track, which tracks were heavy, the odds on any horse you cared to name.

"I bet heavily and often. That was the problem; I hardly ever won. Nobody did; it was a mug's game just like your Josephine said cards were. I knew that but I couldn't help myself. My salary as an actuary at Fidelity Life was pathetic, but I enjoyed the complicated calculations I had to make reducing peoples' lives to theoretical numbers of probability.

"Everybody in the office knew I was into the gee-gees. Half the staff came to me for tips. I didn't mind. Strangely enough most of my tips paid off or so they said. I wish mine had but I have to admit most of my bets seemed cursed. Even if the nag was leading by two lengths you could guarantee the bloody thing would trip on the home straight."

Colin interrupted. "Surely you must have backed the odd winner?"

Ambrose looked up and down the street as though expecting race horses to come galloping around the trees in full flight for the finish line. "We must go," he said lamely as though ashamed of burdening Colin with his story.

"Forget the skip, mate." Colin interjected. "Tomorrow's another day. We're self employed now, remember. We can do what we like."

"Yeah," Ambrose continued, "I had the occasional big win. Of course, I couldn't help bragging about it and I guess my gambling cost me any chance of promotion. Fidelity Life officers were expected to be above all that sort of thing; most of them were.

"My missus put up with my ways. She wasn't happy but she let me off the hook putting it down to the disappointments of life; no kids, dead end job, no future. She said it lent some excitement to our dull lives. Without the occasional flutter she thought I would become morose and bitter. The missus was a real brick, putting up with a second rate husband like me. She was like housewives from her mother's era. You know, stoical and never a word about leaving. There were many weeks when her meagre wage as a night desk clerk at the local hospital kept our body and souls together.

"One Friday night after work I was walking to catch the bus home flat broke except for a few dollars, not enough to put on Crackerjack running in the fifth at Trentham the next day. I did something I rarely did; stopped at the newsagent and bought a lotto ticket. I didn't notice it had jackpotted to seven million dollars.

"One evening a few weeks later the missus saw on the tele that someone had won it. I'd forgotten I'd bought a ticket, and the missus certainly didn't know, but her wistful comment that she wished she was the lucky winner reminded me to get it checked during lunch hour the next day."

"Don't tell me you won the bloody thing," said Colin looking sceptically at Ambrose.

"I did and I didn't," Ambrose replied. "Let me explain. The newsagent staggered. I thought he'd had some kind of fit. Then it dawned on me that maybe I'd won. When he recovered the newsagent explained I had won, but second prize. It was my turn to be shocked but in a disappointed way because my accountant's brain was telling me, if I had won, the interest I would earn would be almost $1 a minute every minute of every day, night and day which came to just under $1500 a day. And I was already mentally spending it.

"It wasn't until I was outside the newsagents about to head back to the office when, even though I was disappointed in missing the jackpot, the realisation of what had just happened hit me. I thought bugger Fidelity and made a beeline for Smith & Caughey. It took the last of my cash but with a fifty grand ticket in my pocket I thought 'what the hell.' The missus really deserved a little something from the perfume counter and I knew her favourite was Obsession."

"I could tell you were a decent bloke, Ambro," said Colin. "Trying to do the right thing eh? No wonder she stuck by you. Did your little lady appreciate the gesture?"

"That I'll never know. After I'd got the perfume I had no money for the bus. I showed the ticket to a taxi driver and said I would pay him if he took me home but he said 'no bloody way' and took off. By the time I got home it was dark and there were no lights on in the house. I thought that a bit strange because the missus always had a hot meal ready when I came home even when she suspected I'd stopped off at the bookies on my way."

"Uh ho, she'd done a runner and here was I under the impression that your missus and you were solid."

"I was under the same impression." Ambrose hung his head then quietly said, "She'd topped herself. Head in the oven, gas on full. Wonder the place hadn't gone up in smoke."

"Jesus Christ." recoiled Colin. "I'm so sorry, mate. I had no idea."

"Well, it's all history now as you said. Anyway, the fifty thou I spent on liquid painkiller helped me get over blaming myself. So did the money from the house or what was left over after everything was squared away."

"So that's how come you ended up on the skips?" Colin looked sympathetically at his friend.

"Yeah, mate; that's how. I never went back to the insurance company and I never so much as read a Best Bets again let alone waste my readies on a nag."

Ambrose brightened up and laughed briefly as though embarrassed at having revealed so much of himself to Colin.

Just then, as if the occupant of the house on whose wall they were sitting had been waiting for Ambrose to finish his story, the front door crashed open. A tall woman in a pale blue suit that matched her hair marched across the lawn towards them.

"Clear off you two," she shouted. "I don't want your sort around here. Up to no good I wouldn't be surprised."

"Christ! It's Mrs Thatcher," shouted Ambrose almost falling backwards off the wall as he made the sudden transition from his past.

"Josephine!" Colin exclaimed, shading his eyes against the sun.

"Josephine?" blurted Ambrose. "I thought her name was Margaret."

"Colin?" said the pale blue woman.

"Hey, that's a coincidence, Col," said Ambrose. "Her name's Colin too."

"No, mate, you've lost the plot. This is my ex, Josephine." Colin spoke patiently as he made the introductions. "Josephine, this is my mate, Ambrose."

"Charmed, I'm sure. I see you've gone into a different type of junk now?"

Josephine gestured at the supermarket trolleys.

"You could say that," Colin replied cautiously. "At least I'm making an honest dollar now. No more cards, no more gambling."

Josephine looked sceptically at the two skip men. "Looks to me like you've both gone down in the world."

"Ah, Mrs, don't let appearances fool you," spoke up Ambrose. "Your husband, pardon 'ex,' is a master at this game. And there's more to it than meets the eye," he added sagely.

"What, you're not just a couple of down and out scavengers then?" she replied sarcastically.

"We may be scavengers in a manner of speaking," said Colin with an air of dignity. "It's what we turn our junk into that counts."

"And that would be...?"

Josephine let her question hang.

"Treasure, of course," piped up Ambrose.

"Speaking of treasure, you look as though you've found yours," said Colin, gesturing at the mansion.

"I would have agreed with you up until about four weeks ago," Josephine said bitterly. "Strange you turning up here like this because I've had cause to think about you and our kids a lot lately. I left you and now my husband has left me; sort of one-all you might say. The bastard took off with a bimbo half his age and left me with nothing."

"You should get half of everything, shouldn't you?" Colin was indignant. "After all, when we split I gave you everything, not just half."

Josephine laughed. "Everything of nothing, if you recall all those years ago, my dear Colin. This one is a bit cleverer than you were then. The house and everything in it is counted as non-matrimonial property because he inherited it. Plus I was stupid enough to sign a pre-nup."

"Good job our kids have made a better job of their lives than we've managed," said Colin. "What sort of business is your husband in?"

"Antiques and collectable paintings, mostly. The house is full of them. Some worth a lot. I advised him on the paintings and turns out I've got a very good eye." She added sadly, "I'm being evicted the day after tomorrow."

Colin and Ambrose looked meaningfully at each other then Ambrose spoke, "You wouldn't consider a couple of reformed gamblers for partners would you?"

"What do you mean? Partners in crime? I might think about it if it means I get to keep what's mine. Come in and have a cup of tea, but push those trolleys round the back of the stables out of sight. This is a pretty up-market neighbourhood in case you didn't know."

"Oh, they're just a front while we scope jobs," said Colin. "Tell you what, I'll go and fetch the van while you make us a cuppa. Then we can have a chat."

Colin took off briskly while Ambrose parked the trolleys then joined Josephine in the kitchen. The kettle had hardly boiled when Josephine let out a squeal and said, "My god, when you said van I thought you meant something smaller than a bloody great truck."

Ambrose got up and leaned on the bench beside her at the kitchen window and looked out proudly as his mate carefully backed the large van bodied eight-wheeler down the drive.

"Good driver is Col." Ambrose looked meaningfully at Josephine. "Good truck too. Side and rear hydraulic lift doors make loading a breeze. We're upmarket now."

He paused and when he spoke again, the rising inflection in his voice made a question of it.

"Swallow everything in this house no trouble at all."

♦   ♦   ♦

The Ballgame of Love

"Oysters?" gasped Amy.

"Yes, oysters... and asparagus," said Dr Philmore.

"But, Dr Philmore, I hate the slimy little things and asparagus is stringy and horrible," said Amy. "And it makes your, um, ah, you know, wee smell."

"That's as maybe, Amy. But if you want to improve your libido," said Dr Philmore, "you must follow my instructions and eat oysters and asparagus at least once a day."

"But I don't want to improve my libido." Amy blinked coquettishly. "I just want to catch a nice man."

Dr Philmore looked over the rim of his glasses at the grossly overweight Amy as she sprawled, overflowing the chair. He put his head in his hands, elbows on the desk and said, "Have you considered losing weight then?"

"'Course I have, can't you tell?" replied Amy. "I go to the gym three times a week. Ladies only, of course."

'You might go to the gym three times a week, lass,' Dr Philmore thought, 'But I bet you have Kentucky Fried Chicken four times.'

"Well," he said, "If you want to catch a man you need to lose weight and eating oysters and asparagus as well as going to the gym is a good place to start."

"If you say so, doctor. In fact I'm off to the gym right now as soon as this consultation is over."

"That's very good, Amy. I hope you keep it up," said Dr Philmore, thinking, 'Fat chance you repulsive creature.'

Amy struggled to her feet and wobbled and wheezed her way out. Dr Philmore hastened to hold the door wide open and said as she squeezed through, "I hope you remember my advice. Oysters and asparagus, Amy. I'll see you again next month."

♦

Amy waddled the short distance across the road to the city gym whose logo of an anorexic androgynous figure surmounted by the words 'Svelteness is our aim, slenderness our game' was prominently displayed above the entrance. Amy puffed unseeing past reception into the member's only area. Some of her gym girl-friends were already there preparing for the session. They wore garish Lycra designer gym gear.

"Hiya girls," trilled Amy. "I've just come from Dr Philmore's. Wooee, what a hunk!"

The girls, who resembled beach balls with fat little protuberances for arms and legs, simpered and giggled. They gathered around Amy as she struggled out of her sweaty street clothes to become a beach ball.

"Tell all, Amy," they chorused. "What did you get up to in his room, you saucy little monkey?"

"He wants to go out with me."

Amy did her version of a pirouette, sending the iced water dispenser flying.

"He said he really fancied me."

"Go for it, girl," bounced back the beach balls. "Those skinny men like a well-built girl like you."

Seven minutes into the power aerobics class Amy staggered to the side of the room, her previously pink and lime green Lycra now sweat-soaked dark red and sea green.

"I've had it," she croaked, "I'm going to get changed then how about we all go over to Maccas and I'll tell you all about Doc?"

◆

"I'll have an oyster and asparagus burger, please."

Amy had remembered the doctor's instructions.

"Sorry, never heard of those sorts of burgers," replied the spotty youth in an oversize Macca's uniform.

"Oh good, I mean, never mind," giggled Amy. "In that case I'll have a double Big Mac cheeseburger and triple fries and large size coke please."

The other beach balls pitched into similar size meals, spraying part-masticated food indiscriminately as they ate and chatted. Amy's encounter with the doctor was far from their minds as fast food took centre stage as a topic.

The automatic doors at the entrance to the fast food emporium slid open. A large man, rotundly oval and bald, and remarkably like a rugby ball stood in the entrance and surveyed the room. He wore black shorts, working boots and a singlet bearing the legend 'You Need Leather Balls to Play Rugby.' His stare alighted on the beach balls and Amy in particular.

He swaggered his way to the counter and ordered a double Big Mac cheeseburger, triple fries and a large size coke. Amy, mesmerised, all thoughts of Doc Philmore cast aside, heard the rugby ball ask for the identical order to hers.

"Spooky," she said to the girls. Desperate to make contact and with no clue of anything else to say she waddled alongside, beach to rugby ball, and said, hoping for a negative answer, "Would you like to share mine? Seems we both like the same thing."

"Yeah, what's that?" replied leather balls without irony, unaware that a similar taste in food would be highly likely among customers of a fast food outlet.

"Why, Big Macs, of course."

The rugby ball, captivated by Amy's bouncy brashness, briefly considered his options then said, "Sugar, I'll stick with what I've ordered. Driving my truck makes me hungry."

"Oooo, a truck driver!" Amy squealed. "How exciting."

The truck driver nodded and, scooping up his mountain of food, patted Amy on the head. Amy was briefly alarmed as the action set off a series of seismic-like waves through her body, which set her bouncing up and down just like a real ball.

"Come on, sugar," the trucker said. "Come outside with me and I'll show you something real special."

"Bye girls," trilled Amy with a cheeky wave of her stubby arm.

Outside, in the truck stop area, stood a monstrous gleaming eighteen wheeler festooned in chrome and lights.

"That's my rig right there," pointed the trucker, becoming slightly less oval as he puffed his chest with pride.

"Awesome!" cried Amy. "I just love a big Mack!"

♦   ♦   ♦

Drunk Night Driving

Sergeant William Walker of the Franklin area police highway patrol sat in the dispatcher's room listening idly to the radio chatter, much of which emanated from the wider Auckland City metropolitan area. Franklin, on the city's outskirts and once a rural district had over the years become less so.

A despatch operator brought him a cup of coffee.

"Why so gloomy, Bill?"

"I've copped night duty every night this week and it's rained on every one of them and that's bad enough," the Sergeant replied. "Now it's Saturday night and you can bet the drunks will be out and I'm so very sick of them."

"Well, you never know. This might be the night nothing happens," said the operator in an effort to cheer up Bill.

"Yeah, right; and pigs might fly. I'd better patrol out towards Karaka where the partygoers coming back from the city seem to fall off the tarmac. Thanks for the coffee, mate."

♦

Richard held Joss's arm to steady her as they made their farewells as gracefully as they could.

"Christ, it's bloody dark and wet out here," slurred Joss, "there's no way I'm driving."

She stumbled down the front steps of the restaurant where the party was winding down.

"You drive, Dicky, I'm way too sloshed."

"Hey, I've had a few too you know, you selfish bitch. You said you'd be the sober driver. And don't call me Dicky; you know, my names Richard."

She *is* a selfish bitch, thought Richard. He hadn't wanted to come to this party, another of Joss's 'office' parties that real estate agents seemed to think necessary to keep morale on the boil. He had come on the condition that she wouldn't drink much so she could drive home. Then he could anaesthetise himself against the incessant braying about property portfolios, killer deals, who was getting a new kitchen or who had just come back from or was setting off for some exotic overseas destination or another.

◆

Sergeant William Walker spoke to the ambulance officer who had just arrived.

"Male and female, cuts and bruises, nothing serious, just another bloody driver over the limit. I've already breathalysed them and they've both consented to bloods."

"Righto, Bill, I'll go and patch them up. You'll want to have a chat with them after?" asked Jim.

The St John's paramedic, like the Sergeant, had attended more drunk driving crashes than he cared to remember. Both had developed a professional respect for each other that expressed itself as friendship on and off duty.

"When you're ready, mate."

Bill watched the St John's man help the injured couple off the wet grass into the brightly lit ambulance. He had a quick word with the tow truck driver about the quickest way to extract the wreck from the ditch. To make sure the traffic was still moving he cast an eye over the rubber-neckers crawling by.

Seeing that everything was under control Bill allowed himself to relax for a minute while he waited for Jim to finish his patch-up work. He knew Jim wouldn't muck about; he, too, would want to be getting home out of the dark and wet night.

Although this was just another incident, quickly forgettable, Bill couldn't help his simmering anger at the stupidity of drunk drivers dragging him out on such a night. He mulled over which approach to take with the driver when Jim was finished. Bill decided that seeing they were mature, well-dressed people driving a flash car he would treat them with icy indifference overlaid with a bit of contempt. When all was said and done people like them should know better; a hell'uva lot better.

He had a little smile to himself at his decision as he thought back to the night before last when the only difference had been that the driver was a young guy. Then he had adopted the scowling, frightening heavy cop approach in the hope of scaring the kid into wising up.

"Sometimes it works," he sighed.

♦

Joss felt as though she was waking from a nightmare-filled sleep as she became aware of water dripping on her face. Or was it blood? With a start she realised the car had crashed into a ditch. She scrambled out to find Richard sitting dazed on the wet grass.

With lights flashing, a police car drew up. A tall traffic policeman emerged wearing a rain slicker and shone his torch on them. Joss could see in the flickering light he was a Maori and handsome in an official sort of way. He quietly and politely asked them if they were all right, to which they nodded.

"All the same," he said, "the paramedic will check you out. Then I'll ask you a few questions. But first, blow into this."

When the St John's man had finished cleaning up the injured he gave the nod to the policeman who climbed into the back of the ambulance, rain water dripping off his slicker. He got out his notebook.

"Now then, madam, who was driving?"

"He was."

Joss pointed at Richard.

"She was."

Richard pointed at Joss.

The cop sighed, and attempted in vain to stifle his exasperation. He dropped his professional persona and, full of fury, said, "I haven't got time for this shit. You pissheads are all the same!"

Then he clipped them both round their ears.

◆

Jim, busy at the ambulance's forward cabinets tidying away his instruments was not really listening because he'd heard it all before. That is, until he heard the slaps and the follow-up gasps of the slapped. He deliberately kept his back to the trio hoping Bill hadn't gone too far, wanting to avoid being a witness if he had.

"Jim, can you have another look at these two?" Bill called. "The scrapes on their thick heads seem to have opened up again."

The two drunks sitting there as stunned as their brains, rendered lethargic by an excess of alcohol, were processing the fact they'd been struck on the head by a policeman.

Richard, the first to recover, spat out indignantly, "You can't hit me; that's assault."

He peered ineffectually through the blood trickling again into his eyes.

"What's your number, officer? I'm not standing for this, especially from a bloody Maori. I'm a Rotarian and on committees."

Joss, the spark gone completely out of her, wiped blood and snot in a smear across her face.

"That's right," she snivelled. "Dicky's a big shot and I'm a real estate agent and we're going to have you for assault."

"Unless you forget about our little accident here tonight. I could even throw in a little koha for the cuzzy bros." Richard had a cunning look on his face, rendered foolish rather than triumphant by the scratches and blood.

The policeman said nothing. He paused as though considering their offer, though he was in fact pondering the sadness of how latent racism frequently emerged when alcohol loosened civilised restraints. He was glad he'd clipped them one. He briefly considered adding a charge of attempted bribery before dismissing the prospect of a full-on court case with all its paper work. He looked at Jim busy placing sticking plaster on the cut above Richard's eye.

"What do you reckon, Jim?"

The St John's man glanced up at the policeman.

"About what?"

"These two twerps reckon I assaulted them, then they had the cheek to try and bribe me. They'll need you as an independent witness, especially as their breaths and, I'm pretty sure, their bloods will show they aren't exactly reliable."

"Drunks eh? Pain in the arse. They must be dreaming." Jim grinned. "Anyway, you've booked them and I've patched them so I'll be off to casualty with these two. Have you radioed for someone to pick them up?"

"Yeah, the paddy wagon'll be waiting. Going to come as a bit of a shock when Inspector Wiremu informs them they'll be spending the rest of the night cell-side." The officer stared at the two offenders. "We'll see who's a 'bloody Maori' then!"

"OK, Bill." Jim chuckled. "Hope I don't see you again tonight."

"Me, too," laughed Bill. "See you at tomorrow's barbie though, as per."

Bill watched the ambulance pull away. Well past midnight now and the traffic had dwindled away to nothing. The tow truck had gone with the wreck. Bill reached into the window of his patrol car and switched off the strobes and doused the headlights so only the park lights gave their muted glow. He realised even the radio chatter had ceased.

He leaned with his back against his car and revelled in the silence. He felt as though he was the only person alive on earth. Rare as it was, that feeling of aloneness thrilled him and his mood lifted. As he looked up and down the empty road and the silent dark farmland he was relieved to note it had stopped raining, and there were bright stars where before there had been blackness.

He tossed up whether to head back to the dispatcher's ordinary coffee or detour up to the all-night truck stop at the top of the Bombays.

It was a no brainer. Bill spun the big patrol car into a u-turn and headed up the Bombay Hill to where he knew Justine, uni student by day, was behind the counter.

♦   ♦   ♦

Book Fair Battles

I was sick of it. I mean, I'm not a small bloke, though not big either. I've been told I'm a typical Kiwi bloke, you know; average height and stocky like a rugby player. You would think I'd be able to hold my own in a crowd, especially as I took care to wear those boat shoes with the inch-thick soles that give me that little bit of extra height, just enough to almost reach six foot.

Most times it works; I have no problems at footy matches, at the track or down the pub. People defer, unless they're bigger than me. Generally speaking, I find my fellow Kiwis are a polite lot.

Not so at book fairs. You'd think people who read books would be extra polite. Yet a book fair turns the meek and mild into cunning ratbags. Kids included. The little buggers have no qualms about standing on my boat shoes.

Middle-aged and older ladies adopt the ploy of total concentration on the books. They hog the inside running and don't give an inch so that big blokes like me have to give way and lose our place closest to the table edge.

Academic types muck about like it's a library, placing their bag full of books on the stacks effectively preventing anyone else seeing what's on offer, while they study the fly leaf of another mouldy old book worth all of a dollar. Earnest types of both sexes rush about with big cartons filling them up and getting in the way as they crouch in the aisles endlessly rearranging their booty checking they haven't doubled up.

As for the types who bring back-packs. Well, I ask you, why would you wear a back-pack to a book fair unless you were going to use it as a battering ram to clear out your competitors? Invariably this type is the larger frumpy female who already takes up more than her fair share of browsing space. As she reaches to snatch a book she has no shame about twisting and turning so that the large pack on her back acts like a kind of pendulum batting away everyone in her path. The threat of injury keeps browsers well back allowing the frump clear browsing ahead. Very hard on us blokes with our in-built sense of chivalry and fair play.

At the last book fair I was at I was just about to give what I thought was a child a nudge because she wasn't moving fast enough, flicking through every stack, when I saw she was grey haired. Not a child, but a little old lady who barely reached my waist. She could have been my grandma if it wasn't for the way she kept baulking me and other blokes who got in her way. My grandma was far too polite and caring to be so rude.

I gave the little old lady a push anyway, a sort of 'accidental' jostle to make it seem like an accident. The little old lady responded with an elbow flick that caught me in the groin and caused me to step back and lose my place, which filled immediately with a couple of yummy-mummy types with carry-all bags -full of kids' books.

As I recovered my breath in the no man's land that is the aisle between the book laden trestles I glanced up to see the little old lady demonstrating her elbow trick to the two appreciative yummies. They must have seen the whole episode judging by how quickly they had dodged into what had been my space. The little old lady turned to point out to her companions where I'd been standing behind her and I was gob smacked to see she *was* my grandma.

I slunk off and headed for the automotive section where I knew blokes like me would be nursing their injuries, including pride. I didn't want Grandma to know her cover had been blown. She had been nothing but sweetness and kindness to me all my life and as I pretended to peruse a tattered copy of *Big Rigs Down Under* available for fifty cents, I tried to come to terms with the fact she was as vicious as all the other females in the room; ruthless when it came to dominating the inside track.

That's when I decided that enough was enough. I was sick of being an also-ran, a book fair wimp, a literary loser. I was going on the offensive. As long as Grandma didn't get hurt.

I cast a surreptitious glance at my fellow automotive browsers either side. Could they be the types to opt in on a joint operation? I wasn't much encouraged by their air of down-trodden resignation, like refugees forlornly cast into limbo. I checked the entire room and sure enough it was mostly men consigned to no man's land and sidestepping the myriad of busty females laden with books who made no effort to avoid the men. More than once I saw a weedy, sandal wearing type go down bowled over by books as the carrier marched on. The poor bloke never stood a chance against the marauding book hounds. I mean, what sad fool wears sandals to a book fair?

The hounds (I'm tempted to call them bitches, but I don't want to give the wrong impression) worked in packs and, mysteriously, all seemed to know each other and be on the best of terms. All the book fairs I'd been to over the years I'd never seen another bloke I knew nor even spoken to one unless to mumble apologies for a minor infraction. Yet the females jabbered away to each other, held up books for one another's approval and swapped life histories and holiday plans all the while flicking simultaneously with left and right hands through two stacks of paperbacks at once.

I have to say that as a result of my assessment of the crowd, which I'd never done before, being more intent on the books than on my competitors, I noticed that there weren't many, if any, good Kiwi bloke types like me. I mean, none of them looked capable of changing their own engine oil. I couldn't see myself calling them 'mate' or 'pal.'

I was pretty sure I was a Kiwi bloke because everyone called me 'mate,' even the shop assistants in Smith & Caughey when I foolishly let myself be dragged in there by my then girlfriend. The guys down at the garage called me 'mate' and so did the old boys at the recyclers. Apart from the tosser at S & Cs I think they really meant it and I returned the compliment. My real mates also called me 'mate;' but I'd never seen them at a book fair and over the years I'd kept my book fair addiction as my little secret.

My offensive might have to be a solo assault. My mateship musings had given me an idea. At the very next book fair if all went to plan I was going to strike a blow for Kiwi manhood and at the same time pick up a few bargain-priced, hard-to-find books from the back catalogues of geniuses like McMurtry, Lodge, Boyd, Parker, Oates, James, Simon, Bryson, Chandler or Block to mention a few. Or even a well-thumbed edition of the *Mammoth Book of Erotica*.

♦

When the next big book fair rolled around I was ready. This was the biggest in the book fair calendar, organised by the Lions and held in the big indoor sports arena over at the Mount. Usually I avoided the opening rush having had some unpleasant experiences involving personal injury and some explaining to do when I was accused of male on female assault. A no-win situation for the male book fair aficionado that I had no wish to repeat.

This time, though, I'd arrived early and parked right outside the main doors. I'd come in my old Holden ute that we used as a farm hack. Obviously once it had been new, but years of abuse and neglect had reduced it to a rusty wreck that if my mate at the garage hadn't been a mate would have seen it fail its warrant ages ago. I was pleased to note that not one of the Jags, Beemers or Range Rovers arriving later took the vacant space either side of my ute. The first part of my plan was working.

Eventually a lady in a disabled-stickered Daihatsu snuck in. The old chook hopped out in a way that didn't look disabled to me. Before jogging sprightly away to join the ever lengthening queue she looked daggers at me as if disabled parking rules applied on Sundays.

I lounged nonchalantly behind the wheel and turned away to watch with interest the occupants of the van which had drawn into the disabled space on the other side of my ute. A bossy female type was struggling to assist a young man into the wheelchair she'd removed from the back. I'd seen this sort of book fair ploy before; using a wheelchair to clear a path to the best books. For all I knew the poor sod in the wheelchair wasn't even disabled. I mean, even if they were why would you bring someone who looked like they couldn't even hold a book, let alone read one, to a crowded book fair?

The queue stretched back right along the front of the hall and disappeared around the corner of the building. I had a little chuckle when I saw someone point out my old heap and shake their head in disapproval. Could have been something to do with the 200litre drum of pig swill I had roped on behind the cab.

Just before 8 o'clock opening time I climbed out of the cab, stamped my steel caps a couple of times as though to make sure my filthy pair of overalls were comfortable, but really to make sure the frumps at the head of the queue were watching. I sauntered towards the double doors aware out of the corner of my eye the watching crowd shrink back to let me in without a word of protest. I was so used to the smell of cow and pig shit and stale milk and god knows what else that my benevolent smile and unanswered good morning greetings were genuine.

The double doors swung open and the Lions' ladies nipped smartly aside as the horde surged forward, flowing around my slower moving person like water around a rock in a fast flowing river. What is it about book fairs that brings on a frenzy to be first? I mean, there's always another one and even the one you're at is hardly likely to run short of books. And we're not talking major expense here.

But I didn't mind being overtaken by a few, amongst whom I was amused to spot the supposedly disabled old lady from the Daihatsu and also the wheelchair duo whose bossy pilot should have taken up a career as a Formula 1 racing car driver. I hoped the poor sap in the chair didn't suffer from motion sickness.

But there it was before me, second only to the heavenly sight of a large library to which you have a valid card; rows and rows of books laid out on trestle tables. Books on every possible subject, fiction by every known author all stickered to indicate their price. What sad souls sticker these books? I mean, don't they have a life because there must be thousands if not hundreds of thousands. I didn't care about sad souls or anyone else as I worked my way

73

trestle-side down one row after another, not once thwarted by any of the annoying types that had made my book fair browsing such a misery in the past.

Except there was one runny nosed coughing kid, who evidently had lost his ability to smell, who got in my way a couple of times until a gentle tap from my steel caps saw him off howling. I kept an eye out for Grandma, but I was pretty sure she wouldn't be at this one because it was a Sunday. I would have been sunk if she was there because she would have been impervious to the ripe farm odours that kept the wimpy city slicker types well clear.

All too soon I had an armful and even some stuffed in the large pockets of my smelly overalls. I may be just your average-sized Kiwi bloke but I felt ten feet tall as I made my way to the check-out table. I noticed that the four or five Lions ladies manning the check-outs pulled back, shrinking away from my disgusting smell and appearance. I had no choice but to approach the one diminutive lady left.

Gobsmacked again; it was Grandma. Luckily I'd put the *Mammoth Book of Erotica 2009* with the others in my pockets, fully intending to hand them over at check-out. As I extracted the others I carefully left *Mammoth* hidden where it was; no point in upsetting that sweet old lady. We've all got secrets it would seem; hers a violent streak, mine a predilection for cheap soft porn.

"That'll be $14.50, sonny," she said, giving me a wink. Not bad for a dozen books.

I gave her a ten and a five dollar note and a kiss on the forehead.

"Keep the change."

I'd come of age at last.

At least where book fairs are concerned.

◆   ◆   ◆

Sunset at the Adventurers Rest

Sir Robert McPherson

I knew I was lost, but I couldn't remember from where or for how long. Anyway the sun was warm on my back and I thought I would keep strolling along enjoying myself. Then I noticed a little girl staring at me while her mother was talking on a cell phone. I could see straight away that the little girl was unwell.

I had only just asked her if her Mummy had taken her to the doctor recently when the mother rounded on me, calling me a dirty old man and a lot of other things.

When I saw the police car coming slowly down the street I thought they were going to give me a ride home again. This time they took me to my doctor, goodness knows why. Then I was taken to the City Hospital by ambulance and put in a ward with a lot of very troubled souls. I tried to help as many as possible, but the Ward Sister was caustic and initially told me not to meddle; an instruction I chose to ignore, which, to give her her due, she came to appreciate.

My nephew David turned up a week or so later. I was surprised to see him. Even though he is also my godson I had hardly seen him since I retired and even less since Angela passed away. I could not get on with him, but my dear Angie smoothed things and insisted we help him financially whenever his business went through its frequent bad patches.

♦

David McPherson

The call from the police had come as a shock. I should have seen it coming, but business problems diverted my attention. Although that was the first time the police had called me, they said it wasn't the first time they had found Uncle Robert wandering; the other times they had just taken him home.

75

This time, apparently, a young mother had reported seeing an old man with his fly open talking to a toddler on Park Street. The police were apologetic, but a complaint had been made and they had to act. Uncle Robert, once Professor of Paediatric Research at Royal Edinburgh University Hospital, was taken to the secure Mental Health Assessment Ward at City Hospital; a nightmarish place that seemed not to bother Uncle at all.

Uncle said he had noticed the little girl had a yellowish pallor that the mother wasn't yet aware of. He was merely asking if she had other symptoms typical of jaundice. Even though he was blithely unaware of his state of dress, happily lost wandering the city streets, his mind, when it came to children's ailments, was as sharp as ever.

At eighty-six he had occasional lapses of memory. This latest lapse had landed him in the Sunset Rest Home for the Aged. I was fortunate to get Uncle Robert in. Left to City Hospital's discretion they would have released him into a secure facility where paedophiles were incarcerated.

I visited him as often as I could, about once every second or third month. I would have liked to have visited more, but I was busy at work.

My wife never liked Uncle Robert, thought he was a stuck-up know- all who should have helped me more than he did. Although she wasn't above name-dropping his knighthood when it suited.

I could see straight away that Margaret Hatcher, or Maggie as she liked to be called, was a wonderful manager of Sunset Rest Home, no-nonsense and efficient. When I was looking for a suitable place for Uncle Robert I observed how she liked to serve at mealtimes and how the 'inmates,' as she called them, seemed to think highly of her.

She made Uncle welcome, making sure to address him as Sir Robert this and Sir Robert that. Uncle settled in nicely; said he didn't mind being there at all, quite enjoyed it in fact. With that comforting news at the back of my mind I wasn't too concerned that, despite my best intentions, I was unable to visit him for a few months.

Maggie took me aside when I finally managed to pay a Sunday afternoon visit. She expressed concern that Sir Robert was upsetting some of the other inmates; guests, she corrected herself. Apparently, he was not at all happy with the food, accusing her of short-changing them, not providing any entertainment and even of turning down the central heating.

I couldn't believe Maggie would be so unkind. I reassured her I would have a word with the old boy.

♦

Margaret Hatcher

I love these old people - or most of them. One or two could be a bit of a trial, like that Sir Robert McPherson. Mostly they keep out of my staff's way.

I pride myself that I provide a safe, warm and homely place for these oldies to spend their last years.

My two most important employees are Matron and Cook. Matron is especially vital to the smooth running of the rest home because her nursing training complements my background in accountancy. Cook has the knack of economising where necessary.

Sometimes we don't see eye to eye about the menu as food is one of the biggest expenses in a rest home. Besides I feel it is important for the health of the residents not to over indulge.

Helping with serving the midday dinner gives me the chance to inspect Cook's offerings and make any little adjustments if she is overly generous with her portions. Saves on waiting staff, too, and makes me feel closer to the old dears. I like to address each resident by name.

"Here you are, Mabel, a lovely pumpkin soup; this mince will cheer you up, Bill; fried potato for tea later, Gwenda; you won't need that apple, Ida, as you've got no teeth; hope you've got enough, Sir Robert."

I leave them to their slow mastication and return to the kitchen to ask Cook to hurry them along so as to clear away before afternoon visiting time. I consider it unnecessary for visitors to see our residents eating dinner, which might invite unjustifiable criticism of the menu.

We encourage visitors to leave early before their loved ones tire. This means we can serve dinner leftovers for tea and give the staff an early night. After tea most of the residents used to retreat to their rooms for a bit of peace and quiet.

Now I notice that Sir Robert and a few others stay on in the main lounge to play cards, so they say. I have tried turning the central heating down, not as a cost-saving measure, mind you, but to encourage them to retire to the sanctuary of their rooms, for their own good naturally.

I've overheard the staff talking about how some of the inmates are dissatisfied. About what I can't imagine. Until Sir Robert arrived I had little trouble here. I frown upon emergencies and we have few demands made upon the staff.

Or me for that matter.

Now there is a whiff of rebellion in the air. Matron and Cook profess to know nothing, but I sense something brewing besides the tea we serve.

If I see so much as a hint of trouble I intend insisting that sycophantic prat of a nephew, David, remove Sir Robert from my establishment. No inmate is going to disrupt the efficient running of my business.

◆

Sir Robert McPherson

David said that Sunset was the best rest home available with a vacancy. He may be right; I don't know. I wasn't given the chance to find one for myself.

I don't mind being in here. It means I don't have to cook for myself anymore and people come along and tidy up and so on. My dear Angela would have liked it; almost like being in an hotel. I do get a bit cross at having to ask permission to go for a walk, but they let me go out of the grounds as long as a staff member comes along.

The staff are kind, especially Matron and Cook. The lady who owns the whole thing is another story altogether. She is a mean old biddy who doesn't have an ounce of charity in her. Cook and Matron try and sneak little treats by her for us. But she has eyes like a hawk and not much gets past her. The staff call her 'Mrs Scrooge' amongst themselves when they think the residents can't hear.

Just because I forget a few things occasionally doesn't mean I'm a half-wit. I can see what's going on and I'm not going to tolerate it. Now that real half-wit of a nephew of mine thinks Maggie Scrooge is an absolute paragon of rest home virtue. She might have him fooled, but me and my friends in here know what's really going on.

David took me aside during his last visit and asked that I don't 'rock the boat' otherwise Margaret will insist alternative accommodation be found for me. I know to David 'alternative accommodation' means living with him and his wife; an eventuality to be avoided at all costs. No need for me to let him know yet how much I agree with him.

Our Maggie is taking everybody for a ride; the health department, the staff, my friends, the paying families and me. Good Lord! Fancy telling me to toe the line as though this is some sort of concentration camp. I'm going to hatch a little plan to put Madam Maggie Hatcher in her place. I know Bill, Mabel and Ida and probably Cook and Matron will want to be in on it.

♦

Margaret Hatcher
I always look forward to lunchtimes as a chance to show my staff and inmates that I care for their welfare. Gives me an opportunity to have a break from the accounts as well.

Cook has done a magnificent job, excelling herself in economical food preparation. The soup could be nothing but hot water, it's so clear. I sip a teaspoon full and the salt in it gives it a nice flavour. I instructed Cook to make the main course a small portion of baked beans on toast as I considered three courses more than generous and besides the inmates would find the soup filling. Dessert is entirely adequate with a slice of stewed pear and a dash of custard.

Although I'm loath to praise needlessly I congratulated Cook on a job well done and push the first of the lunch trolleys into the dining room. I usually get quiet satisfaction from the appreciative murmurings that greet my entrance but today there were none.

In fact the place is empty; not an inmate in sight. I am flabbergasted and shout for Cook. She professes to not have a clue as to everybody's whereabouts.

"Find Matron," I command.

Cook takes her time so she must know full well where everybody has gone.

◆

Sir Robert McPherson
Ida's teeth keep falling in her shandy and we all laugh uproariously, Bill plays the piano, Mabel and I dance a jig. Matron beams as she helps serve everyone drinks. She declines to imbibe herself saying she ought to keep sober to drive us back in the mini-bus.

The noise level rises in The Adventurer's Rest as people rediscover long-suppressed sociability.

I am content with the happy look on everyone's faces when a dinner is served of roast beef and Yorkshire pudding with steamed vegetables followed by fresh, diced fruit salad, pavlova and ice cream. Afterwards while the fire glows and flickers, we sing the afternoon away until Bill can play no more.

On the way back in the minibus to 'face the music,' as Matron laughingly put it, we decide to make this a regular outing. Matron said she would have to hire a bigger bus because all the guests and probably some of the visitors would want to come next time.

When Cook smiles enviously at us on our return and explains that Maggie Scrooge had retreated to her penthouse with instructions that she not be disturbed for any reason whatsoever, I knew we had won a small but vital victory in our constant battle to keep our dignity.

My years of involvement with the health services meant I knew just who to drop a quiet word to about conditions at the Sunset Rest Home should the need arise again.

Nephew David, not surprisingly, seems to be more sympathetic to my point of view since the possibility of my having to live with him and his wife reared its ugly head.

Every evening after the last resident drifted off to bed three of us - Cook, Matron and I - repair to the kitchen where we drink a wee dram of best malt as a toast...

'To life!'

♦

Epilogue

Still and silent, with dust motes drifting slowly in the solitary shaft of sunlight, the room whispered of sadness and loss. Linda, although she had carried out this task many times before, was aware of the room's melancholy message. Cleaning a room, preparing it for its next occupant, a room that had been home, sometimes for years, to a dear old man or lady unwanted by the world made her sad.

As she desultorily waved her feather duster over the worn furniture she thought about the pleasant old chap she had known only as Robert. She had called him Bob once but noticing his slight frown of disapproval had never called him that again.

He had been popular with the staff right to the end. Even the owner, Mrs Hatcher, shed a tear, though Matron told her that Robert and Mrs Hatcher used not to see eye to eye.

The old man only had one picture beside his bed. She was his wife, he told Linda. Sometimes when she came into his room in the morning to clean he would be lying still asleep with the picture clasped to his chest.

He never had any visitors as far as she knew. Except for a rare visit from a man whom she understood to be the old man's nephew. Linda stayed out of the nephew's way because he had no manners, unlike his uncle. Robert was always upset after he'd had a visit from his nephew even though Linda did her best to chivvy him out of it.

As she dusted along the mantelpiece she came to the lovely chiming clock, the only possession of Robert's still in the room. Linda recalled it had caused trouble with a few of the other residents who thought its chimes too loud. She had glanced at the clock many times over the last year, chatting to Robert while tidying his room. Now she bent to look closely at the inscription on the face and read 'To Sir Robert McPherson, KFC, On Your Retirement from the Grateful Staff of the Royal Edinburgh University Hospital, December, 1986'.

Then Linda noticed an envelope tucked underneath the clock. Gently she lifted it up and pulled out the envelope. After all, there was no one left to resent her invasion of the elderly gentleman's privacy. She opened it and began to read the contents.

After reading for a few minutes she had to sit down, overcome with a great sadness. The contents of the envelope revealed who the old man had been in the prime of his life. She realised that the man she had been cheerfully cajoling and chatting with had been a great and wonderful person, knighted for his pioneering research into paediatrics and cancer treatments for young people and further decorated for his leadership of the Royal Edinburgh University Hospital.

Just as she began to read, a newspaper article folded around a photograph, obviously of a happy family, the loud call of the Matron jerked Linda back to the present. She hastily tucked the envelope into her tunic and rushed out of the room to start on the staff toilets.

Sir Robert was forgotten for the moment. But surely not forever.

◆　◆　◆

Eric and Ann, Adam and I

Adam and I became friendly with Eric and Ann while we were at university. I met Adam, who soon became my boyfriend, at the Student Union where we'd both volunteered to help out in the backroom doing whatever but mostly, it seemed, processing mail-outs.

Eric and Ann, already a couple, turned up a year later just when the Union was going through a well-publicised hard time because the President had been caught with his fingers in the till. Eric and Ann were welcomed and hailed as the organisation's fiscal saviours.

I suppose they deserved the accolades because they were both studying economics and politics and, as it turned out, they *were* saviours of the union, steering it back into solvency.

Although I wished them well I remember whispering to Adam (mindful of our student flat's wafer-thin walls that might not actually have ears but certainly hid our earwigging flatmates) that I felt a little bit miffed at the attention bestowed on Eric and Ann before they'd done much at all.

We'd been stuffing envelopes and licking stamps for a year without being offered, as a reward, even a soothing beverage for our sticky tongues. Adam rolled on top of me, and uncaring of listening flatmates, said in his normal deep voice, "Forget about Eric and Ann. You can soothe my sticky tongue anytime."

That's what I loved about Adam, apart from back then he was dead sexy. Still is, really. He didn't seem to feel envy or even notice that he was being taken advantage of. He got on and did what had to be done and sometimes before I even realised he'd started something he had finished it and made a good job of it, too. Yes, sometimes he could be a bit of a bore when he was rabbiting on about foundations or load-bearing walls or backfilling and whatever.

He graduated with Honours as a civil engineer. I studied art history. After we got to know Eric and Ann we had endless friendly arguments about the merits of our chosen courses of study. They with their clever rhetoric and fast wit usually won the debate about the relative worth of our professions.

After we all graduated Adam got a good job with the planning department of the Wellington City Council and I became art teacher at Girls High. The other two immediately took off on high-flying careers: Eric as an economist with Westpac and Ann as an economic adviser to the Treasury. Soon they both became spokespersons for their organisations and appeared regularly on TV.

Adam and I were no longer planets in their solar system. They soared ever higher, impervious to the thin atmosphere at the centre of power's glittering galaxy. We only saw them once or twice a year for dinner parties.

We learnt early on they were indifferent to the fact we had children. The subject was quickly changed if either Adam or I mentioned any of our kids' latest achievement or even if they had suffered a reversal. So we took care not to venture into that seemingly taboo area.

It never occurred to me or Adam to appoint them as godparents to any of the kids; they seemed so very unsuitable and besides, for all we knew, ambition wasn't the reason they had no children. Maybe they couldn't. If so asking them to be gods would have been too cruel.

We were well surprised when Ann announced she was 'in the family way.' I said to Adam as I wiped my face clean of the cold cream I forlornly hoped would slow the ageing process, "Do you suppose they've only now figured out where babies come from?"

Adam lowered his book.

"Who cares? Don't know why you bother with that stuff; you're as beautiful as the day we met. Come to bed and I'll make you feel as young as way back then."

Oh, that man! No wonder I still loved him after twenty years and three kids. Maybe that's why we had so many kids. We knew all too well where babies came from.

Getting used to Eric and Ann as older parents was a bit of an ask. Ann must have been over forty when she had Erica, Eric a couple of years older. They'd beaten the biological clock only just before the alarm went off to ring time's up. The unrelenting tick of the clock meant Erica had to be their only child.

I suppose, then, it was understandable that they should name her after Eric. But I couldn't help thinking it was so naff, so typically Tinakori. What a scream. The highflyers were forced to spin out of their galaxy like rogue asteroids to come down to earth with a lump. Naturally Eric and Ann insisted they were happy with that and a child was what they had wanted all along.

Adam and I had married soon after leaving university. Our first was born a year later and our third four years after that. My teaching career might have been stillborn but I revelled in my new role as mother and homemaker.

Mary, our youngest, was in her second high school year when Erica was born and Brian, the eldest was in his first year at university. Hugh, our middle child, was nominally in the sixth form but really enmeshed in sports of all kind.

While our kids were growing up Eric and Ann evinced zero interest in their progress. Progress it was, I'm proud to say. Brian is a studious character with a wicked sense of humour. He was dux at their school and coped with university science with ease. Not that it was all plain sailing, but he rose to every challenge to the extent that he is now an astro-physicist with NASA doing exactly what Adam and I aren't quite sure.

Hugh wasn't as academic as Brian, but he has an uncanny ability to excel at any sport. He won every high school trophy worth winning, even against older boys. No need to go into his achievements since; they are there for all to read every Sunday in the sports pages.

Mary, our sweet Mary, powered her way through high school, although it is fair to say she had her path smoothed by her two brothers preceding her. Nevertheless with her musical and athletic talents she made her own mark. Music won, and when she turns twenty-five next year she will be the youngest ever appointed as lead violinist in the Wellington Symphonia.

We had long grown accustomed to Eric and Ann being childless. It was an understatement to say that we were surprised when Erica's imminent arrival was announced. What we shouldn't have been surprised about was that you would have thought Ann's pregnancy and Erica's birth was the second coming. Whereas my three productions had passed seemingly unnoticed we had to endure ad nauseam descriptive detail on the progress of Ann's pregnancy.

Although I was proud of my kids it never occurred to either Adam or me to crow about them to other people, except their aunts and uncles and grandparents. The kid's achievements were theirs; they were well recognised by their friends and peers and teachers too. Naturally if somebody asked I would tell them the latest as briefly as I could.

Ann resigned from her consultancies to become a full-time mother. She rang me, it seemed weekly, with news of Erica's latest accomplishment. Ann had enrolled Erica for gymnastics and ballet at the earliest allowable age and had been extolling her achievements ever since. Apparently she was a child prodigy at both disciplines.

A couple of weeks ago Ann phoned to ask if Adam and I would like to come along and watch Erica compete in her school age competitions the following Saturday morning. To be honest I wasn't too keen after putting the hard yards in with our own offspring.

I said to Adam, "Don't think either of them ever came to watch our kids."

Adam aimed the remote at the TV and held the bedclothes open invitingly, "Come to bed, honey, and don't fret about them. Maybe people will think we're young grandparents. Do us good to mingle with youngsters again since our lot flew the coop."

Even now after nearly thirty years married that man can still take my breath away. He always looks on the bright side. He either doesn't see or chooses to ignore the bad in people.

Even so I was still a little resentful of giving up my Saturday to watch other people's children do their thing. I'd been there and done that for twenty years and was getting used to having my life back.

We turned up on the Saturday morning and met Ann and Erica on the hall steps outside. Turned out Ann had to rush off to a hair appointment she didn't want to break as she and Eric were attending an important function that evening. Eric couldn't be there at all due to work commitments.

Suddenly we were premature grandparents. We took the bewildered little girl's hand and gently steered her towards where she was meant to be with the teacher in charge. We sat in the spectator seats and waited for our new charge to perform. After the build up the child had been given we were expecting Olga Corbett and Dame Margot Fonteyn all in one.

To our sorrow Erica was the least accomplished performer that morning which eliminated her from the competition. The poor girl even toppled over while attempting to do a hand spring on the low bench. Her fourth and final attempt brought laughter from the crowd of spectator parents.

Afterwards Adam and I collected her from backstage and wiped away her tears. She was inconsolable saying she hated everything including her mother and father. Adam and I had never been faced with such an emotional outburst from our children so we had a quick consultation on how to handle the situation.

Reasoning that what worked for our kids when things weren't going well would work for this lost soul, we took a hand each and swung her gently along.

"Come on sweetheart, let's all go and have a nice cream tea."

As though she was the only person in the world that mattered to us right then.

Well, she was.

♦ ♦ ♦

Elmore Ffucked.

At last, the signal that told me to start my mission - the single word 'go' in the 'Camels for Sale' column of *The Sands of Time*. This, the only English language newspaper in Baghdad and well-known as a conveyor of coded messages by everyone in the terrorist industry, on both sides of the fence.

I had been waiting for months for this chance to strike back at the Al Qaeda terrorist organisation. I knew from *The Sands* where and when the leadership was meeting. All I had to do was blow them to smithereens. Or presumably, in their case, paradise.

◆

The organisation known as Forum for Universal Christian Knowledge or FfUCK for short, although many operatives referred to it as Ffucked, was a private contract outfit funded by religious fundamentalist churches across the USA, espousing peace and goodwill to all men, but not yet. They specialised in in-country offing.

Apparently demand for their services was escalating, especially since the Secretary of State had decreed that local Arab firms could compete with Americans in the tender process for reconstruction contracts. Seemed like a nifty way to eliminate the competition, get a little edge, so to speak, and even blame it on insurgents.

I was not particularly experienced in this type of security work. In fact, before coming to the attention of Ffucked I had been fired from the Little Rock, Arkansas, Police Department for a self-defence shooting of a swarthy Arabic looking type. He turned out to be a Saudi Arabian diplomat seeking directions. There was no way I could've known he was reaching for his American/Arabic phrase book when I'd told him to step out of the car and assume the position. Needless to say this was picked up by the press who always like to kick the cops when they're down.

Luckily the sergeant was also my cousin and he said he'd write me up as an honourable discharge and wipe the offed raghead from my record as long as I quit of my own accord. It was a no-brainer, especially as this redneck from an outfit called FfUCK had already been enquiring after any likely recruits.

Ffuck hired me almost two years ago to carry out security tasks such as eliminating threats against the Homeland. Or they might have said Fatherland.

Whatever.

When they interviewed me for the job they asked me if I had ever shot anything in the desert. I said yes, thinking of all the rattlesnakes me and the boys used to splatter for fun when there wasn't much going on in the crime department. I'm not sure that was what the redneck who was the head honcho had in mind. I got the impression he would have been more impressed if I had a few notches on my gun belt. But as much as I'm pretty sure he would have approved of my incident with the Saudi I couldn't very well mention it without getting cuz into deep shit.

Truth was neither me, except for that one time, nor any of the boys had ever shot our weapons in anger on the job. Except by mistake this other one time, when an old vagrant well known around the Rock as Alcy Alec jumped out of a dumpster me and the boys were having a good time using as target practice. The rounds made a hell'uva racket ricocheting off the dumpster whining out into the desert. I got such a fright when up popped Alcy's scary one-eyed face with his wild grey hair frizzed up like he'd been fried by the electric chair. My trigger finger sort of froze on full auto and I loosed off a volley that the sergeant kindly wrote up in the day book as a 'legit discharge of weapon while on duty.'

What with one thing and another on paper my record with the LRPD was cool. I was proud of it and sorry to have to leave the department. Not my fault the Ffucked redneck didn't dig a little deeper. I was glad to step from one job into another. Admittedly I would miss the boys and the sergeant and the steady pay check. In

91

my new job I was to be paid on results; half before each offing, half afterwards.

Although I had never done enforcement work on a commission basis before and wasn't sure how it would work, without a doubt this in-country thing was a big step up into the enforcement industry big-time and I was determined to be a success at it.

So far things hadn't been going too well. I had already assassinated three Arab looking types and each time it turned out to be a mistake. The first one was an employee of Telecom Iraq who was reconnecting phone lines in a roadside cable box on the main highway half way between Al Basrah and Baghdad. I thought he was planting a bomb. He also happened to be a Christian and a prominent member of the Iraq Catholic Church. The Pope was upset and demanded restitution from Ffucked, or it would be!

Naturally my team leaders were pissed and demanded their money back. I promised that, in the immortal words of that crazy good Gerry Rafferty song, I would 'get it right next time' and I would cut them a deal; I offered to do the next for half price.

My next victim wasn't my fault either. I had kept a suspect under surveillance using infra-red night vision scopes. The suspect lived in the old quarter of Baghdad in a three story block of flats in which some beautiful women also lived. When I got a bit bored surveilling the suspect I could perv at these girls. Being on the third floor they thought nobody could see them when they disrobed from their burqas and revealed the pretty face behind their yashmaks.

One night I was intent on a particularly foxy lady, indistinct from a sack of spuds and any other on the street but, shucked of her useless ethnic costume, a dead ringer for Penelope Cruz. So intent that one night I failed to notice a swarthy type coming up behind me. He gave me such a fright that as I swung round I involuntarily shot him.

I scarpered and had to exit the country before the authorities put two and two together and came up with my number. The suspect, who evidently could also do the math, now fully alerted that a shooting outside his abode probably wasn't a coincidence went to ground and so far has never been seen again. I kept my part in this cock-up quiet from Ffucked and duly reported the suspect had disappeared.

My third victim was a case of mistaken identity so could hardly be labelled as my fault either; all towel-heads look the same to me. The American Embassy had notified Ffucked that a shady character had been attending their functions squiring the ambassador's daughter. Via the usual newspaper I got the green light to check him out. It did puzzle me why an older Iraqi chef on the Embassy's staff would appeal to an American gal but he had the correct name so I clipped him. How was I to know nearly every second rag-head's name was Al-Lamy.

Ffucked let me off the hook on that because they admitted they hadn't fully briefed me that it wasn't necessarily a crime against the Fatherland – pardon, Homeland - just to be an Arab. They actually had to commit some sort of aggressive act or suspected of doing so sometime in the future before it was OK to rub them out.

I was mightily pleased to hear this because during my days with the LRPD I'd always found the old idea that guilt had to be proven a fricken' time waster. For the life of me I couldn't see what was wrong with incarcerating suspects for being suspects. What was good enough for President Bush was good enough for me. Unfortunately it would seem, not for the suits at LRPD or even my sergeant cuz.

◆

This Al Qaeda bombing job was to be my last chance. Ffucked would tolerate no more fuck-ups. Blow this, so to speak, and I would be lucky to get a job on the executive of the National Rifle Association of America helping perpetuate Charlton's memory.

Well, I'd read the 'go' word, so it was time to put my plan into action. I'd decided to give them a taste of their own medicine. I would load up a handy car with 400kg of high explosive wired to go off when the hood or trunk was opened. I made sure the petrol filler door was included in the circuit. I knew that the thieving Arab bastards would be all over it minutes after I left the car. They wouldn't think it was booby-trapped because they would have seen a Westerner, me, exit the driver's door. There would be a bit - correction, a lot - of collateral damage but them's the breaks.

The day of the Al Qaeda leadership meeting arrived and I carefully set off, with circuit activated, in my time bomb on wheels loaded with enough killing power to take out a city block. As I got to the main road I noticed the car was short of gas. Some low-life thieving Arab must have siphoned some out before I'd connected the wiring. Luckily there was a Q8 gas station right there so I pulled in and handed the pump jockey a ten dinar note. No point in filling it up.

I watched in the mirror as he moved around to the petrol flap...

♦　♦　♦

The Bach

Jim Jamison, known to the locals as Jimbo, inherited one of the baches that previously had a view across the sand dunes to the sea. His grandfather built the first bach, more a shack, out of whatever materials were at hand. Like the axe with three new heads and two new handles, the bach had undergone many transformations and modernisations over the years. But it was still a bach like the others either side of the sandy track that long ago became Oceanbeach Road.

Jimbo knew he was privileged to have parents and grandparents who treasured the old place enough to pass it on to him, and which he in turn would pass on to his kids. In a way the bach had been the reason he'd met and married Sal. She, too, had been coming to the beach with her parents, who had a bach one street back from Oceanbeach Road, for as long as both of them could remember.

At first a childish Christmas holiday thing their romance, like a fire on slow burn, gradually flickered until Jimbo's forced absence as a cadet on Sanford's big fishing boats fanned their infatuation into the deep and lasting affection their marriage had become.

♦

Cynthia and Royce Fortescue-Smith were convinced they owned the ultimate status symbol. They called it The Bach. In fact it was anything but. A huge expanse of glass and steel, three stories high, a lift to whisk guests from the atrium on arrival to the living room that opened out to magnificent sea views on the third floor.

The mansion, for that is what it was, blocked their neighbour's view of the beach and sea and completely dominated all those more modest, traditional baches. Three had been demolished to make way for the Fortescue-Smith's architectural gem.

Royce liked to think he had 'made it.' He had amassed a fortune as a merchant banker. He frequently pontificated on his banking role to an audience captured by social decorum into hearing out someone who had 'shouted' them a drink. He dismissed the blank stares from the drinkers at the bar of the Cosmopolitan Club as coming from ignoramuses. The drinkers in turn couldn't see where the 'risk' was in sitting at a computer compared to the real world in which they made their living.

Cynthia and Royce liked to invite acquaintances down from the city for the weekend, relishing how their guests, expecting a real bach, were nonplussed by the grandeur of The Bach. Royce took delight in relating how money will always win when it comes to beating those who relied on the Resource Management Act to stop projects like The Bach.

All except the crassest guests found a reason to decline a repeat invitation. Most were embarrassed by their loud host lording it down at the town's Cosmopolitan Club.

◆

It was sometime in the early fifties, when Jimbo's father owned the bach, that the track had been widened and tar-sealed. To do so a kink was put in to connect Oceanbeach Road with the new road curling around from the estuary.

The fact the Jamison bach ended up on the inland side of the road didn't worry anyone. Sections were generous and the baches small. The sea views were hardly affected, whether on the seaward side of the road or not. There were no fences and everybody treated each other's sections as public property. Access over the neighbours section made getting to the beach more of a social occasion than a chore.

Jimbo and Sal never invited anyone. They didn't have to. There were always kids, grandkids, friends and neighbours (one and the same thing) coming and going. They'd retired to the bach permanently years ago. Jimbo would dispute the 'retired' bit because he was still in partnership with his old skipper Tony in a couple of deep sea trawlers working out of Tauranga. Jimbo maintained that the occasional trip to the city to attend to business affairs counted as work therefore he couldn't be retired.

It was common knowledge that Jimbo had been inside. In fact Jimbo made no secret of it. He saw the trouble he and Tony had with fish quotas and other bureaucratic nonsense as part and parcel of the trials and tribulations of starting up their fishing business again in the face of ruthless competition from the big company outfits.

Jimbo regretted that the media saw fit to drag up this part of his past again. He couldn't see how his early years in business was relevant to his, and the majority of the townspeople's opposition to the destruction of the character and amenity of their beloved beach.

◆

Police Sergeant Bill Walker had transferred down to the beach nearly twelve years ago after he'd got sick of pulling drunk drivers out of ditches in South Auckland. The beach was a sole charge station, totally different from where he'd been, although extras, including some from his old Franklin area, were drafted down for the summer months.

Bill thought he might have a bit of trouble mixing in with what he assumed would be a rich bach-owning bunch of whiteys.

His assumption proved completely wrong. Jimbo, by then retired and a permanent resident, was the first to break the ice over a few beers at the very public Cossy Club. If the Sergeant was aware of Jimbo's brush with the law he gave no sign of it. The two families, Sergeant Bill, his wife Justine and their kids often barbecued together, usually at Jimbo and Sal's place because it was closer to the beach making it easier to take the grandkids to splash about in the sea.

Even during the height of the protests against the Fortescue-Smiths, with Jimbo prominent among the protesters after their appeal to the Environment Court had failed, the Sergeant had remained neutral like the conscientious policeman he was. Didn't

97

stop him having a drink in the club with the protesters or barbecuing with Jimbo and Sal. Justine never said much anyway, always conscious of her stutter.

During one of those late summer barbecues Jimbo noticed Bill holding Justine's hand gazing quietly at the behemoth that was the Fortescue-Smith's palace. Lights blazed, spilling out of the floor-to-ceiling glazing, so that it resembled a passing cruise ship, which would have been all right except it wasn't moving, as though it was anchored permanently offshore.

Bill looked up at the stars, usually crisp and bright in the beach's evening sky, and lamented the light pollution that meant he saw none. For the first time since the hint of unwelcome developments had hit the seaside town the Sergeant's bias revealed itself in the observation he made to Jimbo that their view of the sea and access to the beach was gone and they couldn't even see their familiar Southern Cross.

♦

Jimbo was nursing a beer and propping up his usual stand-up table at the Cossy Club. He finished up a cell call from Tony about nothing much just when the Sergeant pushed through the big swing doors. The locals nodded a greeting, accustomed by now to seeing the Sergeant in his blues.

He tried to sidle by the Fortescue-Smith crowd and failed to conceal his irritation as one or two Hooray Henries that he'd never seen before heckled him with smart comments that he'd heard a thousand times.

Jimbo had signalled for the barman to bring over a handle by the time the Sergeant reached his table. They turned disgustedly away from the Fortescue-Smith rabble.

After the Sergeant took a long draught he casually mentioned that the Fortescue-Smiths had approached him for extra security for a party they were throwing next month. None of the locals had been invited nor expected to be. Apparently they were bringing down some of their priceless artefacts from their city home as decoration for a photo shoot that was to feature The Bach in a new interior design magazine.

Jimbo tried not to show interest above what the Sergeant might expect. They had known each other for a long time, but Bill was still the law and Jimbo wasn't. All the same he and the Sergeant rarely talked to each other about their jobs so he couldn't help but wonder as the Sergeant began to describe in detail, in a circumspect manner, the artefacts and the security system. Jimbo smiled inwardly as he realised that if by remote chance drinkers on the next table had overheard them impropriety would be the last thing they would suspect.

The Sergeant let slip that some of the artefacts were solid gold. Then enquired innocently if the furnace Tony used for smelting lead weights for nets was still operable in his Tauranga workshop. Jimbo didn't exactly reply, but then he didn't exactly not either.

Without another word passing between them the two friends departed after the next round knowing exactly what each was going to do on Fortescue-Smith's party night next month.

♦　♦　♦

Car Yard Combatants

Schultz Car Sales wasn't much of a business as far as used car yards go. For desperation it probably wasn't different from some of the other yards that lined the state highway leading into the city. Like most of them, a port-a-cabin office perched on piles, as though ready to be taken away when the business folded, was sited along the back fence. The stock of cars exposed to the elements covered the asphalted yard.

The big glossy franchised showrooms had long migrated to the newly-fashionable commercial area bordering the downtown business and shopping district. On dismal windy, wet days the franchise salesmen thanked their lucky stars they had warm bright showrooms to work in with the bonus the cars they were confident of moving stayed immaculate.

Snow, nicknamed for his predilection for wearing white shoes and matching belt, longed to progress beyond Schultz's to one of the big franchises where the salesmen with their retainers were not entirely dependent on commission. Survival at Schultz's meant keeping up to quota, even on a day when the rain pelted down.

Snow and his three cohorts were gathered at the office window gazing forlornly out at the deserted lot in the faint hope that a punter might appear.

"Dunno why you bother coming in on a day like this," he remarked to no one in particular. "Schultzy never bothers."

"Ah, yes," said Brian, one of the other salesmen. "That's because he's the owner and isn't on a quota like us."

"Do tell," Snow said. "Like I've said before we should have a roster, except you blokes are shit scared one of us'll steal a march on the others."

Snow was gazing out the window as he spoke, even as the rain obscured his view. The others had again drifted over to the coffee machine. Out of habit Snow put a trade value of $7000 on a small blue Mazda he noticed draw up in front of the yard. He watched as the Mazda's door opened and the woman driver ventured purposefully into the yard, flipping up the hood of her coat against the rain.

Snow charged out before any of the others could beat him to the punter.

◆

Jennifer saw him coming and her heart sank as she hunched her shoulders deeper into her warm coat as though to ward off the salesman's onslaught as much as the weather.

"How are we today?"

Snow's bellow combated wind and rain.

Jennifer wanted to answer 'Piss off you cretin' to his hearty enquiry. Instead she coolly replied, "All-right."

Snow ignored the subtle rebuff, if he had even noticed the missing 'Thank you.' He launched into Rule 1 from *The Manual on Successful Car Sales Techniques*, known in the trade as the *How To Stitch Up A Punter Manual*, which was to get the punter to agree with something. Anything.

He blurted out the first thing that came to mind.

"Beautiful day isn't it?"

"In case you haven't noticed it is hosing down," retorted Jennifer.

"I, ah, meant it was a beautiful day to purchase a car."

A lame recovery.

"Don't be ridiculous."

Where on earth did these salesmen drag up such bullshit?

Snow dimly realised he'd lost that round. In one short exchange the score was one nil. Who did this stuck-up punter think she was?

But Snow wasn't a man to give up easily. He tried again, moving on to Rule 2: Establish personal contact.

"What sort of vehicle are you looking for, Ms… I'm sorry I didn't catch your name?"

Jennifer parried his unsubtle query.

"That's because I didn't throw it, you fool."

Two nil to the punter.

101

Thoroughly rattled as well as soaked, Snow racked his brains, not an extended process, as he considered his next sally.

Jennifer, snug in her waterproof Burberry coat with matching hood, was well aware that Snow couldn't afford to let a punter escape, especially not while the other salesmen laughed and gestured at him from behind the warming safety of the office window. She wandered to the far corner of the yard where the cheaper cars were displayed.

Snow splashed up alongside to where she was surveying a large old Dodge. He was well aware that it was a rust bucket cleverly disguised with fibreglass and cheap 'blow-over' paint and the motor was stuffed to boot. Now confident that the punter was an automotive ignoramus, Snow was determined to even the score. Boy, he ached to stitch her up in this old heap.

"That's a wonderful motor car, madam, one little old lady owner, a petrol miser; never been raced and in immaculate condition like it just came off the factory floor."

"When did it actually come off the factory floor?"

Snow employed the standard evasion.

"I'll have to check the papers in the office."

For a moment he thought he had evened the score.

"Take it for a test drive while I check."

"No, don't bother with the papers," said Jennifer cheerfully. "I'm not really interested in the Dodge after all. I want to look at that car."

She pointed at a smooth red Alfa Romeo coupe gleaming as though spotlighted in its own shaft of sunlight while all around sat drably dripping in the rain.

Three nil to Jennifer.

By now the bedraggled Snow, his pink shirt and green jacket streaked with hair dye, white belt and shoes turned into a mottled, soggy mess, assumed he was dealing with not only an automotive ignoramus but worse, a tyre kicker.

'Aha,' he thought, 'I've got you now. I'll teach you not to waste my time.'

He neglected to consider the possibility he was kissing a sale goodbye and said as smoothly as though he had been telling the truth, "I'm sorry, it's the Managing Director's wife's car. It's not for sale."

Jennifer shrugged. Casually she wound her way between the cars and out of the yard and home to write up her report.

Four nil.

♦

Snow, as soaked and irate as he had ever been, squelched back to the office. The watching salesmen greeted him with laughter at his discomfort and slapped each other on the back like the good ol' boys they imagined themselves to be.

"You dickhead Snowy," they chorused. "Didn't you know that punter was a mystery shopper?! Yeah, man, she works for the LMVD. You'll see her when you go up there for your disciplinary hearing!"

"What hearing?"

"The one she'll be writing you up for," chortled the good old boys. "Misrepresenting the Dodge and telling her the Alfa isn't for sale."

"Fair enough on the Dodge, but how would she know about the Alfa?" Snow countered plaintively.

Visions of a cushy gig with the glamour franchises faded.

"Because, dickhead, she's Schultzy's ex. Divorced years ago and she knows damn well he hasn't had a missus since. The bitch does her annual check when she's certain Schultzy won't be here, likes to give us, and him, a hard time! She not only knows the *Stitch Up Manual* backwards; she wrote the sequel, *Putting Pushy Salesman In Their Place.*"

Snow sighed.

"Bugger," he said.

♦ ♦ ♦

Saturday Night Out

"Hello, Killer speaking."

I said it as a joke, certain it was one of my mates. We'd had a session in the club rooms after the match and I'd cleaned them up on the pool table. I might be crap at football, but I'm a killer at pool. I had no trouble bouncing that white ball off the cushion to kiss those coloureds into a pocket.

I wasn't planning on going out, but it wasn't unusual for Brian or Mike to come up with a late plan sure to involve drinking and a dead cert with some woman or women seemingly conjured out of nowhere. Invariably the only dead cert about such plans was we'd all end up pissed to the eyeballs and the women would be long gone. That's if they'd ever existed except in those no-hopers' imagination. They could play footy though.

Nobody responded, but I could hear heavy breathing.

"Who's there?" I said a little testily this time.

More heavy breathing.

"Come on, whoever you are," I yelled. "Speak up or I'll hang up."

By now I was convinced it was some jokester of a mate.

More heavy breathing and what - sobbing? My mates didn't sob even when they were acting the goat.

I'd settled down with a book and given Edward Sharpe and the Magnetic Zeros permission to blast hell out of my speakers. So it was only a fluke that I heard the 'phone. Even more of a fluke that I answered it, but then I was sure it was one of the lads and they knew I was home. Normally I would let the answer machine pick up because the last thing I want to be doing on a Saturday evening is sorting out some unfortunate's problem with their hot water cylinder or, worse, their bog.

"Right, that's it. I'm hanging up."

Before I could disconnect a woman whispered, "Help me, please."

"Call back in office hours. I don't do call outs on Saturday nights. I'll talk you through how to turn your water off at the mains then you can call me Monday."

"What are you on about?" Louder now but still uncertain.

"Who the hell are you? What's your name?"

"I am..."

Back to whispering. I couldn't catch what she said.

She tried again.

"I'm trapped and frightened."

"Well, Miss Whisperer, why are you whispering and where are you trapped?"

"They're out there and I don't know where I am. Please help me."

"Look, what can I do? I don't know you or where you are, either. Who 'they' anyway?"

"They dragged me into their car and raped me."

More sobbing now.

"I jumped out at some traffic lights and now they're out there hunting for me, they're going to do it again."

"How did you get my number? Who are you?"

I was a bit desperate by now. Didn't know what to think, let alone do.

"Your advertisement is on the wall of the 'phone box I'm in. Says you do emergency call-outs twenty-four seven."

"Yeah. I'm a bloody plumber if you'd read the whole thing, not your emergency services."

I cursed myself for a fool letting that tasty lady in the advertising agency talk me into telling the world I was available round the clock. Truth was I had plenty of work, what with the rebuild, in regular hours. I usually deleted any after hour calls that the voice mail picked up.

I made a mental note to check Monday morning where exactly Miss Advertiser had placed my ads, then go and rip them down. I'd only consulted her because I was hopeful enough to think spending five hundred bucks would oblige her to me. Like come on a date.

After I'd paid the money over and I'd worked up the courage to ask her out to dinner she came over hoity-toity and said she had other plans.

The sobbing was distracting.

"Hey, shut up a minute while I think."

Miss Whisperer obeyed. Actually she hadn't said a word while I ruminated over the shortcomings of my advertising campaign and crap social life.

"Are you still there?"

Hoping she wasn't.

"Yes, I am still here. Are you going to help me or not?"

Still whispering, but definitely impatient.

I was about to ask her why she hadn't dialled the cops when I thought I could hear something in the background.

"Hold your phone up towards that bell sound."

Now I could hear it. If I wasn't mistaken it was the level crossing bell outside Hornby on the Prebbleton branch line. Trains hardly ever used it these days, but when I was footy training I often ran a circuit from my place in Westmorland up Marsh's Road. Sometimes an endless procession of containers took ages to pass me while I jogged on the spot waiting to cross the line. The strident bell just about drove me nuts as it worked its way into my brain. I guess it hadn't been deactivated like all the others because there were no houses near enough for their occupants to complain.

"Hurry!" She whispered, calmer now. "They're coming closer."

"Hang on there, I'm coming to get you. I'll be there in five."

I started for the door hoping my old banger would start first time for once. I always parked the van loaded as it was with plumbing gear on the drive in front of the garage if I wasn't planning on going anywhere flash.

Of course, the bloody thing wouldn't start. Why would it? It knows I don't go out plumbing in the dark. I popped the bonnet and whacked the starter with the hammer I keep for that purpose in the driver's door pocket and the engine caught first twist of the key.

I was going to take my car. After all, what knight in shining armour turns up to the rescue in a plumber's van complete with ladders and lengths of pipe tied to the roof? But I'd already blown too much time mucking about with the starter. I missed the sat nav though and had a sinking feeling I was shortly going to miss a lot more. Like a working heater and an engine that could propel its occupants at more than sixty clicks. Anonymity without my name and numbers plastered along its sides might be good too.

On the other hand, whoever was stalking the girl might take me for a plumber out on an emergency job, I reasoned. Why else would a plonker be driving around in a plumber's van on a cold Saturday night?

Why indeed?

The only answer I could come up with was that she had a sexy voice and an even sexier whisper. Christ! Us blokes are so bloody shallow. I might have spoken the thought out loud to a non-existent listener. Something I'd caught myself doing lately with alarming and ever-increasing frequency.

She sounded blonde to me, with a gorgeous figure, not too much of anything, except legs. I like legs, long legs. 'To be honest' - definitely out loud this time - 'I'm not fussy as long as she looks how she sounds.'

So ridiculous I snorted. I mean, how can you tell what somebody looks like from the sound of their voice.

I ended the conversation with myself as it became obvious I needed to concentrate to negotiate the wet, dark streets barely illuminated by the heap's pathetic headlights. It didn't take me more than seven minutes to turn into Marsh's Road. Although I knew the area, I couldn't place a telephone booth near the railway crossing. But then when I'm on a training run or driving between jobs telephone booths aren't exactly my focus. Cell phones have rendered them redundant.

I knew the branch line going north next crossed a road almost in the centre of Hornby and I knew damn well there were no warning bells there. So I turned south towards Prebbleton and the industrial area that I guess was the reason for the branch line in the first place. I crept along, unsure of my bearings, through a street rendered a wasteland at night of one-man businesses and barely lit factories.

Two dim streetlights illuminated the dark and dismal shops I guessed was Prebbleton. And there to my surprise was a new glass telephone booth outside the dairy.

Empty.

I cruised up one side of the street and down the other. It didn't take long. I could as easily have parked on the intersection and straddled the railway tracks for all the activity going on in Prebbleton that Saturday night.

I decided to do another circuit, which gave me a moment to revise my poor opinion of my van. At least the poor girl - if there was such a girl - would recognise my name, sign-written along its length.

Nothing moved. Except for headlights further down Springs Road where industry turns to farming. The headlights didn't seem to be coming towards me or, if they were, only slowly.

I was about to embark on another conversation with myself along the lines of 'idiot' coupled to 'wild goose chase' when the passenger's door was wrenched open. Not an easy feat at the best of times ever since a roofing tradie had backed his truck into my door. A person I guessed to be the sexy-voice whisperer tumbled into the cab.

"You are Jelly Villiams?"

Again that foreign accent I'd half-noted on the telephone.

"I must be. That would be Gerry Williams. It says so on the van, doesn't it?"

I was a bit bolshie. My fantasy wasn't working out. The girl was dressed for an inclement Saturday night; not scantily as I'd hoped but quite tasteful and quality. I began to suspect I'd been set up to give a free ride home to a poor student chucked out by her boyfriend from a party.

"You're not a Kiwi, are you? I thought you'd be a blonde damsel in distress."

"I am a damsel in distress, but no, I'm not a Kiwi. I'm Indian. Indian girls are not blonde."

She nodded her head in that manner that confirmed her origins from the sub continent.

"Well, I thought you would be blonde and tall and..."

I was about to say 'gorgeous' when I took a longer look at her and saw she *was* gorgeous. So I shut up.

"Can we get out of here, please? I wasn't joking - kidding, do you say?"

"Sure," I said convinced I'd be taking her back to Lincoln which after all was just down the road. "Where do you want to go, Lincoln or CU?"

"Oh," she said, "already you are leaving me - how do you say? - in the lunch."

I had to think about that.

"No, I'm not leaving you in the lurch. I meant Canterbury University. Do you want to go to Lincoln or C U?"

"Ah, I understand. You are most kind. Unfortunately I have nowhere to go at this moment. But I would very much like to go somewhere soon if at all possible because those monsters might be quickly coming back."

"Yeah?"

I was not entirely sure but I gave her the benefit of the doubt. I banged the van into gear and swung around to head back to the city. Besides I'd noticed the headlamps down Springs Road were closer and the occasional beam of a torch flickered over the waste ground between the dark buildings. Clearly the car's occupants were searching for something or someone.

"That is them. They search for me twice already, but I hide behind shop under some boxes and they didn't see me."

She gave a little sob at the memory of her terror. Maybe this wasn't a wind up. I shifted up into top as the magic sixty approached.

"Do you have a home where I could have a rest and make myself presentable?"

"How do you know I'm not a sexist misogynist myself?"

Sometimes I don't know where such big words come from for a plumber.

"You must have somewhere I can take you. And what about the police? I mean you should report your attackers. Assault is a serious crime in this country."

"Also mine," she said haughtily. "To be truthful those horrible men didn't actually rape me. But they said they were going to. I escape from vehicle."

We were silent for a while as we came into the built up area. I made sure we hadn't been followed by turning into a couple of side streets, like a private eye in a Lawrence Block thriller. Eventually we came into my street, which is just about the cliché for suburbia, newish brick and tiles built to the boundaries and a pool in nearly every back yard. Good for me though; pools are a plumber's best friend.

"No lady or other mans in the house?"

I was charmed by her misuse of my native language, which surprised me because when locals get it wrong I get mad. In a way that's what cost me my first marriage. She wasn't bright enough, kept mispronouncing and misusing words, couldn't write for toffee. All my oh so helpful and concerned mates said before we were married it wouldn't last. They said plumbers were morons not good enough - not smart enough, they meant - for a beauty like Jackie. Trouble was, that's all she was, beautiful, and believe me skin deep ain't enough.

Then she started having a go at me for spending too much of the 'household income' on books. I thought that was a bit rich seeing I was doing most of the household incoming. Beauticians don't make half as much as plumbers and, if they do get a bit spare, end up spending it on themselves to keep looking the part. Not a priority for plumbers.

"So many books," the girl said making a beeline for the floor to ceiling bookcase that runs the length of my entrance hall. "Why do you have so many books? Have you read them all?"

"So many questions. No, I haven't read them all - yet. It's a bit of a hobby as a break from hot water cylinders, sinks and dunnies."

"Dunnies?"

"Karzies, bogs, porcelain, long drops, crappers."

She was none the wiser. Never mind, we'd sort that out another time.

"The books, that's many books for anyone, not only a plumber."

"Yeah, well, I like traipsing around book fairs and second hand book shops. I've got a mate, Jack up north, who's the same. We work as a team building up our collections of rare books. He covers the North Island and I do the South. Jack calls himself the Book Fair Bandit and he's taught me a thing or two like how to beat up little old ladies when necessary."

She cried out in alarm.

"Beat up ladies? Little old ladies!"

"Only a figure of speech."

She didn't look much reassured.

"Luckily we don't collect the same subjects and genres."

I could see from the way her eyes glazed over that was too much information, but she did ask.

It came to me that this entire situation was somewhat surreal, on more than one level. Here was I revealing my predilections for books and book fairs to a strange girl in my home. The girl had apparently been subject to a traumatic experience yet I was telling her about my interests. Interests that, apart from Jack a thousand kilometres away and possibly my mother up the road in Hoon Hay, I took good care to keep private. Not a good look to be a literate plumber.

"Look, I'll show you the bathroom and get you some clean clothes. They'll be too big for you, but they'll have to do."

Too big was an understatement. The leggy blonde of my dreams would have suited some of my casual gear all right, but this girl could get away with nothing but one of my shirts and it would hang around her ankles. She was everything my fantasy blonde wasn't.

Then I softened. Maybe so, but she was a beauty too with her pert - well, everything. Her skin was smooth and dark. In contrast to her tear –streaked face, her long, black hair was clean and silky.

I stopped staring when I realised she was blushing.

"I'll get a couple of my shirts and slacks so you can choose. I'll leave them outside the bathroom door. I'll be in the kitchen making us something."

I backed down the hall, berating myself for babbling and bowing like a schoolboy. She wasn't royalty, for God's sake, and I doubt I'd bow to them. She's just a girl.

I busied myself in the kitchen knocking up a couple of cheese on toasts. Delicious with Mum's homemade green tomato chutney. I'd put the jug on for some instant when it occurred to me that maybe people from India didn't eat cheese for religious reasons. I had no idea what they did eat except curry and rice. I couldn't recall ever seeing anything cheesy on the menu of the Indian take-away in Hornby.

For reasons that made no sense to me I desperately wanted to impress this girl with my culinary skills. I began a hasty search through my cupboards, knowing full well I had nothing that remotely could be labelled ethnic.

She came into the kitchen quietly and said, "What is it you are doing up there?"

I nearly fell off the stool I was standing on so I could rifle through the top cupboards.

"Nothing much. Just checking my food supplies."

I felt a bit of a fool. Moving on, I said, "I don't suppose you could eat some cheese on toast could you?"

"Oh yes, very much so. Especially good with chutney. Do you have chutney of any kind?"

"Does the Queen wear a crown?"

That got a blank look so I added proudly, "Of course; green tomato made by my Mum."

We both jumped when someone thumped on the back door. I flicked on the outside light and peered out the side window of the kitchen. Mike and Brian stood there, gesturing to be let in.

I opened the door.

"What are you two arse - " Oops. Lady present. "- guys doing here at this time of night?"

"The babes we had jacked up and bought drinks for all evening went off with a couple of suits so we decided to call it a night."

Mike was generally the more sensible of the two.

"Saw your lights on and noticed a car with some dudes in it parked outside," Brian chimed in. "Thought you might be having a party without telling us."

He fished a half-bottle of vodka from his coat pocket.

News of the car outside shocked me. I went into the dark front room and eased back the curtain.

"Shit. It's the same car."

The girl gasped from where she had been keeping out of sight behind the divider.

The boys whirled around.

"You *are* having a party, you old dog," said Brian.

"No, no, nothing like that, guys. I'm looking after ...this girl."

I realised I still didn't know her name.

"Yeah, right."

Mike stared pointedly at the girl, dressed in one of my shirts and not much else.

"A very private party with a babe you've kept us completely in the dark about."

"Listen, thickos. This babe...girl called me out of nowhere. Thought I was some sort of rescue outfit. She had been abducted and threatened by those blokes in that car out there. They must have followed us here. Now you know as much as I do!"

"Come on then, guys. Let's sort them out!"

Brian spoke enthusiastically, never one to shy away from a scrap.

"We should call the cops," said Mike.

The girl spoke up.

"Please, no police. Maybe those horrible men will go away."

"If they think you can identify them they won't go away," I said, "And the cops will be overloaded with drunks downtown about now so it might take them a while to get here anyway."

"Those blokes outside think you're here on your own," said Brian. "I'm all for tooling ourselves up and having a go at them. The amount of footy we play we must be fitter than a few lowlifes."

"Yeah, from what the ...ah... girl has said I think they're white-supremists so they shouldn't be too much trouble to knock over, Mike."

"OK, I'm in. After all, there's three of us."

"Four," the girl interjected. Quiet but firm, she was five foot four of steely determination.

"Four it is then," I said. "We'll split up."

I pointed at the girl.

"You, Mike and I will sneak out the back door and jump over into the neighbours before crossing the road around the corner. They'll be watching the house with a bit of luck and won't see us coming down the other side of the street."

I beckoned.

"Brian, you stay by my front door until you see the three of us rush the car then you come out too, make as much noise as you want then we'll smash hell out of their car before they know what's hit them."

I paused.

"Should put the shits up them and if it doesn't and they stand and fight, which I doubt, then you... girl... hightail it back here and you *will* ring the cops."

"OK. This time if worst happens, how do you say, 'shit fly into fan' I will definitely call the police."

"And when this is all over you *will* tell us why you don't want to call the cops."

I was impressed with my own forcefulness.

"And your name," added Mike.

"Yes, your name."

Why did I feel Mike had somehow trespassed on my territory as though I owned the rights to knowing the girl's name?

I crept into my garage, careful not to turn on any lights and grabbed a couple of pipe wrenches for the two lads, a baseball bat for the girl and a length of leftover lead piping for me.

Brian whispered, "Good luck, team," as we disappeared into the night.

I could tell the others' adrenalin was pumping as much as mine as we got into position. I felt like Robert B. Parker's avenging private eye Spenser, even if my sidekicks didn't exactly measure up to Hawke and Susan Silverman.

I signalled 'go' and we charged across the street, weapons at the ready. Brian emerged from the house as planned and within seconds we all laid into the glass and metal of the car yelling blue murder as we did so. I guess we'd got in one blow each when the occupants, now themselves yelling in terror, fired up the engine and shot up the street, their beaten-up car, belching sparks and smoke.

"Inside everyone before the neighbours get nosy."

I ushered the team inside just as a few lights began flickering on up and down my usually quiet and civilised street.

"Wow, did you see us give those skin-heads a go?"

Brian was still high with excitement.

"Lucky for us." Mike was calmer. "If they'd stayed until we'd done some serious damage we'd have some explaining to do with the law."

"Speaking of explaining."

I adopted what I hoped was a stern expression.

"You...girl. First your name then why the secrecy?"

"My name is Serena Nair. I come from Southern India where I am Associate Professor of Agriculture at Calicut University."

She laughed.

"Also C U."

The lads were puzzled, but I didn't enlighten them.

"I am here on exchange with Lincoln University organised by our Embassy to study agricultural irrigation schemes. In our

115

country it is shameful to be involved with bad men. I was in the central city on my own, perhaps a little bewildered by the earthquake damage, and I was looking for public conveniences when mens looking like Nazis started calling me things and then grabbed me into a car."

She sighed and shook her head.

"It was my own fault, but no-one told me such a thing might happen in New Zealand all harmony and green and pleasant. If police involved it would reflect badly on India and perhaps I get sent home in disgrace."

"But you're the victim here," I interjected.

"Women always the victim in my country."

"Well, not here." I spoke firmly. "Anyway, we've sorted out those skinheads and they won't trouble us again. You're safe now."

"We'd better stay just in case."

That was Brian, ever hopeful and clearly taken with the girl.

"No need, but thanks, guys. Couldn't have seen those ratbags off without you."

After the lads left I felt a bit awkward with the girl I now knew as Serena. She seemed perfectly at ease. Now that I had time to absorb her presence and was no longer frightened, I could see she was certainly no girl but more likely close to my age.

"Look, I realise it is late, but can I take you somewhere? Perhaps you shouldn't stay with a single man alone in his house."

I kicked myself for drawing attention to her situation.

"You are so kind but if it is all the same to you I prefer to stay here rather than go back to hotel at this hour."

She curled up in the armchair and I handed her the toastie.

"Perhaps you can tell me exactly what a plumber does? Doesn't it mean you are good with pipe connections, pumps and water supply?"

This was the first time a person of the opposite sex had shown the slightest interest in my job. I could see from the expectant way she studied me that Serena was serious.

"Yes," I said.

116

And all awkwardness evaporated.

♦ ♦ ♦

Study of a Hopeless Case

Barry had seen her before. She must have lived somewhere in the same suburb because he had noticed the girl on a bright red Vespa a couple of times; had given way to her once at the intersection of the main commuter route into town. He knew the scooter rider was a she because long hair streamed back from below her helmet. The jacket she wore couldn't quite conceal the swell of her breasts. Beyond that he had paid her no mind.

Until now. On his way home he slowed his company station wagon to a stop near the knot of people gathered round a still form on the grass verge. A yellow bus sat idling next to the kerb blocking access to Barry's street. The mangled scooter he recognised lay on the tarmac near the back of the bus.

He climbed out of his vehicle and gently shouldered through the bystanders to see a man in bus company uniform holding her head off the ground. Her face was scratched and bloody and she seemed unconscious. As Barry turned to ask if anyone had called an ambulance his question was answered by the rising siren wail of approaching emergency vehicles.

Barry knelt down to help the driver hold her. The bus driver said she was alive and not too badly hurt. Came out of the side road without looking. Couldn't miss her, he said.

Barry saw the injuries to her face were superficial. The bleeding had stopped. Her helmet lay nearby and looked as though it had taken a blow at the back. It had her name, printed crudely in red across the front. Gail. If the helmet had done its job properly she would only have slight concussion.

Now that he'd had a good look he could see she was young, probably only seventeen or eighteen. She was also beautiful in that unsullied way only the young can be.

The ambulance men took her away. Barry pointed out to the policeman that he only lived a few doors down the street and that he could mind the mangled scooter until she or the police decided what to do with it. The policeman took his name and address and helped him lift the scooter into the rear of his wagon.

Joan enquired why he was late, scolding him for ripping the knee of his business suit. Barry omitted describing the rider as he told her what had happened. He didn't have a conscious reason for this. Meant to, but something made him conceal the fact the injured rider was a young girl and beautiful.

Confounded himself even as he spoke. Only the previous weekend at their twentieth wedding anniversary party he had toasted the rapport and trust he and Joan enjoyed. Hadn't mentioned love.

After dinner, consumed as usual watching the TV news, he pleaded work and drifted into the study and closed the door. Joan said nothing, but was sceptical, knowing Barry's job bordered on the mundane. He hadn't brought work home for years.

Barry pondered on the girl. He would go and see her in hospital tomorrow, during his lunch hour. Ask her what she wanted him to do with her scooter. He would tell Joan, if she asked, that he had to find out where she lived so that he could drop it back to her.

He felt a vague excitement at the prospect, which Joan sensed with her usual perception. She mistook it for an unscheduled quickening of his desire, usually reserved for a Friday night towards the end of the month.

At first repelled by Joan's advances Barry managed to enter into the spirit of the mood by visualising the girl and what she might look like beneath her jacket. When they were done he flopped back on the bed silently appalled by his callousness. He turned his back to Joan with a small feeling of shame.

Next morning, shame dismissed, he pecked Joan on the cheek and set off for his commute right on time. Called out to Joan as he rushed out the door that he would ask the police for the girl's name and address. He left the scooter in the station wagon in case he could deliver it after work on his way home.

He went through the motions all morning, which made lunchtime seem like hours away. He wished he had the willpower to actually do something constructive, write a report nobody would read, answer nonsensical emails, send a few jokes. Anything to make the time pass quickly.

Eventually midday ticked around. Barry shrugged on his jacket, waved off his usual coterie, avoiding enquiry, and left the building. He had no difficulty finding her. Hospital staff pointed the way. He was taken aback to find her in a general recovery ward. He had fantasised she would be in a well-appointed single room, like on TV.

The girl was sitting up in bed reading a magazine. Apart from a small bandage on her temple and discoloration from bruising, she looked stunning. The beds either side of her were occupied; one by a sleeping elderly lady, the other by a middle-aged man. The ward was busy with staff going about their duties and visitors chattering.

Barry took a minute, standing just inside the ward door. The business of the hospital flowed around him. She, four beds down on the left hand side, didn't glance up from her magazine even as he approached her bed.

"Excuse me."

Reluctantly she lowered the magazine.

"Are you the doctor come to OK my discharge?"

"No."

Her face registered disappointment. The conversation hadn't got off to the start he'd hoped.

"I've come to find out what you want done with your scooter," Barry stammered.

God, how lame he sounded. Here he was more than twice her age and she, most likely, in a vulnerable state and he with nefarious intent and couldn't get out a coherent word.

In the neighbouring bed the middle-aged man, the same age as himself he realised, spoke up.

"Have you come to take your daughter home?" he enquired.

Trapped into repeating his reason for being at her bedside, Barry amplified his explanation with detail on how he had come to be on the scene of her accident. It still sounded lame.

The girl said for him to drop the scooter at her home address a couple of streets along from his. Her father would help him unload it. Her childish voice and syntax did not belong to the sophisticate he had imagined her to be. It belatedly occurred to him as an unlikely possibility that a beautiful and worldly wise woman named Gail would be trundling around the suburbs on a motor scooter.

She picked up her magazine signalling the conversation was over. The middle-aged man winked at him as though he knew exactly the evil intent that until a few minutes ago had been uppermost in Barry's mind. The man smirked.

"Right little Lolita, isn't she?"

The girl's indifference hurt Barry because he'd thought, stupidly he now realised, she would be grateful and interested in him. He'd be the good Samaritan in whom she could trust and confide. Instead he could see her youth, beauty and ignorance allowed her to be interested only in herself. She hadn't even thanked him, let alone asked his name.

The afternoon in the office dragged on as unproductive as the morning. Barry found himself thinking about Joan. He thought about the Lolita remark from the man in the hospital and was ashamed. Nothing had happened with the girl, but he had desperately wanted it to. If the girl had been a little older, a little brighter, he might have started an affair. Perhaps after all those years with Joan he was open to infidelity.

On the way home he pulled over onto the waste ground near the railway tracks, waited until there was no traffic and dragged the wrecked scooter out of his wagon and over a small bank out of sight. He made a short detour to the block of shops near his suburb and bought a couple of bottles of wine and a bouquet of Joan's favourite chrysanthemums.

He reasoned there was no way Joan could suspect his wayward intent. On the other hand the gifts implied a devotion reawakened by their love-making the previous night. Guilt didn't enter into it. Barry resolved to put carnal thoughts of beautiful girls behind him and be satisfied with whatever Joan could offer him.

Joan didn't respond to his usual greeting on arriving home. The house was silent. Expecting, irrationally, to be welcomed home like some sort of returning warrior, he was miffed at her silence then annoyed as her absence became obvious.

He picked up the folded note from the breakfast bar, perched on one of the stools and read. Joan had gone, tired of his indifference. Gone with the intention of never coming back. If he had shown the slightest interest in her while making love last night, she said, she would have stayed and tried to make things better. The next he would hear from her would be a lawyer's letter.

Uncaring of his fickleness, unaware of his stupidity, Barry grabbed the chrysanthemums, rushed back to where he had dumped the scooter, wrestled it into the station wagon and drove off full of optimism to the girl's address.

♦　♦　♦

Abdul Gets his Shit Together

Abdul had quit Iraq in a hurry. He found out he'd been sprung when he spotted a foreigner lurking around his apartment block. Foreigners were easy to spot; more so those who affected Islamic dress because invariably they got the combination of headgear and garments wrong. The one Abdul had seen hanging around wore an Arabian jubba known as an iman's coat, which is usually worn by clerics and other important officials. He had on a cheap kufi, which barely covered his hair, when he should have been wearing an elegant flowing smagh and egal in the style traditionally worn by desert people.

At first Abdul thought the foreigner was a guest worker hanging out to pick up one of the little boys or even a girl. This had become too common in Baghdad, although not so much since the new so-called Prime Minister had decreed a crack down on that sort of thing. Then he spotted the foreigner had ginger hair, which was highly unusual in Iraq, so he must have been a European. He seemed to be hiding across the road in the grounds the city authorities called a park. Apart from a couple of sickly acacia trees it was more like a dusty dump.

Three nights in a row Abdul came up through the park, circled behind where he knew the foreigner waited and watched him watching. Abdul could see his night vision binoculars tracking men who came and went from the block, some of whom were Abdul's colleagues. The foreigner missed plenty because most of the time his glasses were trained on the window of a woman on the third floor. Abdul could hear the foreigner whispering phrases to himself in an American accent.

"Jesus H. Christ, look at those bazookas. Almost as perky as a centrefold."

The woman seemed unaware that from some parts of the park she could be observed without her burqa. As a good Muslim, Abdul

123

tried not to look, but found the temptation irresistible. More out of shame at his own weakness than for any other reason he rushed at the godless foreigner in a red mist of fury.

Abdul's suspicion that the ginger-haired man was a spy was confirmed when he spun round, whipped out a Glock and fired. Lucky for Abdul he proved to be a poor shot and the bullet passed harmlessly through the outer folds of his dishadasha. The only damage was a small hole that could be easily sewn up.

Clearly shocked and frightened, the American let out a yelp as though it was he who had been hit. He took off down the dimly-lit street, his jubba and smagh billowing out behind him like a lateen-rigged dhow on the Nile.

Even though the spy had left the scene Abdul, as logistics and supply officer for the Baghdad branch of Al Qaeda, knew his time was up. The Americans were stupid and never seemed to learn. Unfortunately this ignorance made them tenacious and dangerous; they would come again.

His area commander promised him passage to London and explained to him he would have to go 'underground' for a while. But once there he would receive untold benefits from the British Government for doing absolutely nothing. Abdul listened with mounting incredulity as the commander endeavoured to explain the 'welfare' system. He'd never heard of it and couldn't believe such a thing existed. He thought it unwise to question why a country so generous towards its poor should be the sworn enemy of his organisation.

Travelling to Britain hadn't been difficult. Crossing into Iran then taking passage up the Caspian Sea was arranged by Al Qaeda to Astrakhan in the Russian Federation. Abdul's new papers said he was involved with the purchase of materials for Iraq's oil industry pipeline replacement, which provided him with VIP status as the Russians hoped to be Iraq's biggest supplier of oil pipes.

From there it was a simple matter to board the Volga river-boat as far as Volgograd then train across Eastern Europe to France. The final hop across the Channel was a little more problematic, but the hierarchy had that in hand too. It meant roughing it for a few nights with the dispossessed in the huge camp that occupied waste land just outside Calais docks.

Passage had been arranged in one of Farsi Transport Company's curtain-siders that brought Islamic clothing for the vast Muslim population in Britain. The Farsi trucks were such obvious targets for the fat, sweaty, lazy, beer-breath British Customs officers that the illegals avoided them like the faithful a synagogue.

What the stupid British didn't know was the pungent smell of the leather goods and untreated fabrics was similar to the smell of the occupants, including the skinniest hidden in the tiny compartment underneath the false floor of the trailer. Sniffer dogs couldn't make the distinction either.

Abdul found himself deposited unceremoniously on the streets of London on a bright, if somewhat cool, morning in May. The border control bastards had given the Farsi truck such a going over that the driver swore that Al Qaeda could go fuck itself and never again would he take a terrorist across the English Channel. Abdul had never heard such blasphemy, nor he himself described as a 'terrorist.' Although he had never actually done any 'freedom fighting' that is what he considered himself to be as a supply officer.

Before Abdul had a chance to ask the truck driver where he should make contact with the local Al Q rep, the curtain-sider disappeared in a cloud of diesel. Knowing himself conspicuous in his dishadasha he made for the familiar sound of humans engaged in commerce. He edged around the corner of a scruffy brick building, the like of which he'd never seen in Baghdad, to be confronted with the bedlam of a street market in full swing. He was relieved that many in the market, stall holders and customers alike, were dressed like him.

He stood observing and let his panic subside. He looked carefully around and couldn't see any of the police his commander said would be on every street brutalising the population, especially Muslims. He couldn't work out who was keeping order. Many of the people appeared jocular, swapping banter with stall holders, then bursting into raucous laughter. Abdul was stunned.

Next instant he was disgusted, watching English girls flaunt themselves in skimpy tops that exposed their navels and shorts or skirts that let him see for the first time the legs of women other than his mother. He puzzled over the fact some of them were black yet seemed English in every other way. He also noticed that he was the only one staring.

One of the blindingly beautiful girls, had she been in Baghdad, would have been arrested by the religious police for public immorality. She acknowledged Abdul's fixation with a two-fingered gesture he thought an invitation until bystanders laughed at him.

Another called out, "Here we go then. Fresh off the boat, eh?"

Abdul was totally mystified. He'd come by truck and he didn't think a stranger could have known about his boat trip up the Caspian Sea and Volga River.

He pulled himself together as best he could while reeling from the cultural assault on his sense of righteousness. Confusingly, he was simultaneously exhilarated by the evidence before him of a freedom he had no idea existed. If his commander had been present Abdul might have asked him how come his organisation was the sworn enemy of such obviously happy and unafraid people who seemed to not even notice there were different races in their midst? No wonder it was so easy to plant bombs.

Abdul sidled up to a brightly-coloured stall that was selling brass kitchen utensils of the kind he had seen made in Isfahan. He hoped the man sporting a fez, even though he was also wearing blue jeans and a white shirt, might be a Muslim.

"Can you help me, brother? Allah Akbar."

"Yeah, mate." The man in the fez gave him a sideways glance. "So is my God great. They're all bloody great. Even yours probably."

"Sorry, brother." Abdul was taken aback. "You are not of the Islamic faith then?" he blurted out.

"Was once, gave it up. Too much aggro. Now what do you want, mate? A nice big, shiny tea kettle all the way from Iran?"

"Most regretfully, sir, I do not need a tea kettle but I was told I would have to go 'underground' when I got to London. Can you help me with this?"

"Is the Pope Catholic?"

Absolutely flummoxed, Abdul tried to make the religious connection in the context of the unfolding conversation. Before he could reply the man pointed down the road.

"Right over there, mate, is the underground. Aldgate Station to be precise."

Abdul looked where directed and sure enough a big red and blue sign on the far side of the market had 'Underground' written on it. When he turned the other way he could see another and couldn't understand how he had missed such obvious signs. He had assumed the underground would be a bit more covert instead of plastered on almost every street corner. He wondered if perhaps he wasn't the only stranger adrift in London and the signs were there to make it easy for everyone new to the revenge business.

Amazed at how people going about their business ignored him, stepping politely aside, not even putting the shoulder in, he walked to the underground station. A tall white man with ginger hair reminded him of the American in Baghdad, but he smiled at him and Abdul smiled back. If the ginger-haired Englishman hadn't been holding hands with another man Abdul was certain the man would have turned and spoken with him. He wouldn't have minded as it was common to hold hands in Baghdad, although never with a European.

Abdul quickly found out that his lack of money prevented him going down the escalator that led truly underground into the bowels of the earth. He hung around the concourse until way past nightfall looking hopefully at anyone who came in dressed similarly to him, desperately hoping the stranger might be his missing contact.

127

He hadn't eaten for more than twenty-four hours so he wandered back out on to the street to find the market packed away. He mingled with the people who seemed to be in a tremendous hurry but in a multitude of directions. He noticed fruit and vegetables half rotten though to him perfectly edible in black bags piled around a skip that was overflowing.

Satiated, he soon found a sheltered spot behind a closed stall next to the public toilets. He turned his refuge into a cosy shelter with the aid of plentiful cardboard. And there he remained for the next week even venturing to the other underground in case he'd got the wrong one.

But nobody approached him. Abdul watched a turbanned man who appeared from nowhere at the same time everyday languidly waving his mop at the white-tiled floor of Aldgate Station conveniences.

"Excuse me, brother. Allah Akbar," Abdul began straight off, anxious to test if this man was a true believer and not a mixed up Islamic Catholic Pope unbeliever like the Iranian brass utensil stallholder.

"Whatever," was all the turbaned man said, which puzzled Abdul as he hadn't said anything much yet.

"I was told the Underground was where my future lies. Yet no one has sought me out to provide this future. Can you help me with this, please?"

The cleaner paused, pondering.

"Ah, you mean underground, not *the Underground*. You need to see this geezer who'll be along shortly with my roll in the hay."

Convinced the man was speaking gibberish, something he'd noticed many dirty people did as they shuffled along, Abdul moved away but kept an eye on the entrance to the conveniences. Eventually a man made important by his high-vis jacket marched boldly into the gents. Abdul followed him and saw him hand the cleaner an envelope. Aha, roll in the hay. Baksheesh.

The cleaner saw him and beckoned him over and said to the high-vis man, "This geezer wants a job underground."

128

Abdul swung around to see who the geezer was. The high-vis man looked scornfully at the skinny, ill-kempt Iraqi in his now filthy dishadasha.

"Got just the thing for you, sunshine. Come with me."

Abdul was conscious he had no means of paying the baksheesh that was clearly required to obtain and hold a job. He used the term he had heard others employ as a mode of respect.

"A thousand apologies, guv'nor. I have no currency whatsoever."

The high-vis man clapped him on the shoulder.

"Not to worry, me old China."

Abdul, puzzled, tried to work out the significance of the geographic reference.

"We can sort out the 'baksheesh' all in good time week by week if you know what I mean."

The high-vis man winked at the cleaner.

So it was Abdul found himself leaning on his shovel deep underground repeating 'Allah Akbar' at every stroke to thank his god for his good fortune in landing a job cleaning sewers in the sanitation department of London City Council Water Maintenance Division. A career previously held by successive waves of Irish, Africans, West Indians, Pakistanis, Indians, Polish and now it would seem Iraqis and other gentlemen from the Middle East.

He had to pay a small baksheesh to the Irish guv'nor who then sent him with a chit to the Indian foreman who assigned him to Sewer Cleaning District 8. Abdul was used to that sort of torturous bureaucratic nonsense so thought nothing of it.

District 8 proved to be in the underground area of Kensington and Berkley Square. Abdul was convinced this new shit smelled fragrant in comparison to the sewers he had crawled through delivering Mk 9 anti-tank rocket warheads. He said so frequently to his workmates who decided he was mad.

He was a good worker even if he opened his mouth too much. He had never had tea breaks before and thought it wonderful to be paid for stopping for a tea break and lunch. Like 'the welfare,' he had never heard of 'unions' before. The union said they had to pause in their work every two hours for ten minutes. None of them could actually afford tea or anything to eat anyway; but Abdul looked on the bright side as he didn't fancy eating while in the sewer.

Abdul usually spent break times guessing which turds were from rich Americans and which were good British turds. There was no way he could confirm his guesses, but it must have been more than coincidence that those from Berkeley Square were mostly long and fat like oversized sausages.

Thoughts of bombs faded as he experienced the joy of consumerism. He bought a compact music system and marvelled at the pure sounds of Mozart and Beethoven extracted from it merely by inserting a disc. Unintentionally he tuned in one evening to a classic hits radio programme and was mesmerised by the sound of bands he'd never heard of like Dire Straits and The Rolling Stones. Singers like Gerry Rafferty, Bruce Springsteen and Bob Dylan held him in thrall as though they were singing directly to him.

Then he bought a 20 inch flat screen colour TV that fitted on the wall of his Spitalfields bedsit and he was lost. He thought back to his old freedom-fighting days and, forgetting Allah, thanked his lucky stars that the ginger-haired American had missed.

While flicking through the CDs at the Aldgate Street market, where his English saga started, he bumped shoulders with a tall African girl clad in a skimpy top unbuttoned enough to reveal the swell of two stupendous breasts and a pair of cut-off shorts that did likewise for her buttocks. By then Abdul was well familiar with English girls' mode of dress and knew to make anything of it was asking for trouble. He knew from her accent she was English to the core when she said, "Robby Williams is crap, inhe?"' as they both bypassed him for a Who CD.

Abdul aware that he had made a connection was flustered and blurted out the first thing that came into his head, "I work in the sewers!"

"No shit!"

"Yes, plenty of shit, heaps of shit, loads of shit, nothing but turds."

He was proud of his mastery of the vernacular.

"All look and stink the same: English, Iraqi, terrorist, Queen or Ayatollah." He added meaningfully, "Black, white or brown."

The black girl laughed at such a unique come-on.

"*You're* full of shit." She grabbed his hand. "Come on, mate. I'll shout you a cuppa."

Abdul was puzzled by her coarse reference to his faecal capacity and pleasantly shocked by her physical intimacy as she held his hand. He was mystified by what 'shout' meant with reference to a cup of tea when she hadn't spoken particularly loudly. Until they were seated in the little greasy spoon next to the market and a cup of hot tea strong enough to stand a spoon up in appeared in front of them.

"I get it. Shout means I pay. No problem."

The black girl grinned.

"Whatever."

♦ ♦ ♦

The Misfortunes of a Ruler of the World

Royce Fortescue-Smith hadn't noticed the bag lady even though she had been there each day for the last fortnight. He strode, nose in air as though avoiding unpleasant smells, along Goldman Street on his way to work in the futures department of Silversteins Merchant Bank. The bag lady recognised Royce striding along; a clear path opening for him through the commuters, miraculously so, although Royce couldn't see that and thought it simply the natural order of things.

He had scarcely spared a glance for the old bag lady, or anyone else, beyond when they got in his way enough to upset the rhythm of his power walk. Then he snarled some coarse obscenity, thrilling himself with his boldness and setting himself up for another day of cut and thrust shuffling anonymous money around the world for margins measured in fractions of cents per. Royce considered the commission he earned on his shuffled billions well deserved.

On Friday morning he had stumbled into the old lady as he barged out of his favourite tobacconists, eyes fixed on the horizon. She went tumbling down the pavement and Royce gave her a kick as he marched past mouthing bad words vaguely in her direction. He failed to make any connection between this minor incident and the fact his day turned out to be the worst he had ever had, losing millions. For the first time he found himself in a negative cash position at the end of the day thus kissing his commission goodbye.

♦

The old bag lady shuffled along, bent and presumably broken. She was dressed in a grubby gaberdine coat that either belonged previously to a taller owner or herself before she shrank. The bag lady was not who she appeared to be but a woman named Justine

Green. Had Royce turned and looked after he'd put the boot in he would have seen the bag lady speaking into a wrist mike.

Justine was an undercover operative from the Society For The Prevention of Grossly Over-Compensated Paper Warriors (SFTPOGOCPW). She was alerting the Society's base operatives in Ponsonby that Royce Fortescue-Smith had set himself up for another bad day at the office.

An aspiring actress, Justine was studying drama at the Auckland Drama School. She had been offered the SFTPOGOCPW gig by her boyfriend Richie Cassidy, an accountancy student. He and a group of fellow ardent anti-capitalists, mostly students, had formed the Society to make life difficult for the high and mighty who manipulated the world's money supply and therefore ruled the world.

Between them and the two computer nerds who also belonged to the Society they had enough hacking firepower to set superpowers on a path of mutual economic destruction. To hack undetected into banking computers was child's play.

Routine surfing through the foreign currency futures trading account of the Silversteins Merchant Bank had brought Fortescue-Smith to the Society's attention. Here was an individual making obscene amounts of money on commission who cared not a hoot what small countries he impoverished in the process. Justine was despatched to assess what the hackers could not; if he had any redeeming qualities of compassion.

If none, then the Society would use the super-ego blindness of targeted individuals to teach them a lesson.

Justine first checked out Royce's domestic situation. She followed him to his house, set on the northern slopes of Mount Hobson. As expected the house was equal to the neighbourhood; faux Victorian, grand and ornate, facing the distant harbour. High walls and a remotely operated five-barred gate kept a pair of Labradors in and kept all visitors without appointments out.

Justine had no trouble transitioning from bag lady to real estate agent, which quickly got her a request to call round from Mrs

133

Fortescue-Smith. Cynthia hinted that she hated the pile and would sell in a flash except it was leased. Justine thanked her politely for her time and made to exit, though not before Cynthia had downed four sherries to Justine's half.

Turned out that Cynthia hated more than the house, she loathed Royce as well. Apparently it had been a long time since they'd shared the marital bed, but Cynthia couldn't afford to divorce the bastard. While this tirade poured out Justine took the opportunity to observe the many fine artefacts gracing every polished surface.

She was especially taken with a series of bird sculptures and a collection of exotic masks, seemingly of solid gold.

◆

Reporting back at Ponsonby HQ, Justine told Richie that she'd seen no sign of any humanity whatsoever in the life of Royce Fortescue-Smith. He didn't treat his wife nicely beyond the material and there was no evidence he supported any charity. He, and she it must be said, were acquisitive in the extreme.

The Labrador dogs were walked and fed by a toady, which despite the fact it provided him with employment counted against the Fortescue-Smiths as laziness. Finally Royce's treatment of unfortunate strangers in the street was appalling, as Justine had found out the hard way.

Justine, Richie, the nerds and a couple of dweebs reeking of pot put to the vote whether or not to teach the merchant banker a lesson. All attempts to tease even a minuscule amount of compassion from the man had come to nothing. Richie was hot on democracy, which Justine admired, though neither realised the relationship between capitalism and democracy is entirely symbiotic.

It was unanimously agreed that Mr Fortescue-Smith, having failed to respond to subtle fiscal stimuli, would have to be shown the error of his ways. Justine had vague and unvoiced thoughts about the gold artefacts. Perhaps liberation could wait for another time when there might be better circumstances to liberate them. Far easier to stick with the tried-and-true hacking game.

The team gathered round the nerds as they altered a point here, added a zero or two there, wiped out one transaction altogether, and diverted another worth a few million into a private account where it definitely should not have been.

Within a matter of days Royce Fortescue-Smith's fiscal position was hopelessly compromised, and his personal accounts revealed systematic insider trading. Richie made an anonymous call to the Fraud Squad and that was that. The nerds couldn't resist embedding a few bestiality porn shots in Royce's computer. After all, as they pointed out, he was a rapacious animal.

♦

Postscript

Justine Green drifted away from Richie and SFTPOGOCPW partly because she developed an intermittent stammer when she had to pronounce the Society's acronym. She never did get her acting degree. She took up surveillance work instead with CRAP, an organisation pledged to make life miserable for real estate agents. A hell of a lot easier to spit that out.

This quasi-police work bought her into contact with Bill Walker, then a South Auckland police constable. Now grandparents, they remain happily married and, by all accounts, very well off.

Richie Cassidy graduated with a Masters in Economics and Accountancy. His interest in SFTPOGOCPW waned as rapidly as his income rose and the Society went into recess. The nerds apparently ensured that any search of records would show no such society had ever existed. Ritchie is slated to be the next Minister of Finance in a National Government. His nickname 'Hopalong' recognises his propensity to jump on whatever cause is popular of the moment.

Royce Fortescue-Smith went to jail - but not for long. In a rare mistake the nerds had embedded, instead of porn, innocent pictures of mating animals from the World Wide Fund for Nature website.

Royce declared his interest in conservation and built on rehabilitating his public character to show he was a man of compassion who had strayed. No harm done and he'd make it up to society.

His ego prevented him making any connection between his behaviour and subsequent market reversals and his conviction for fraud he put down to carelessness.

His wife, Cynthia, impressed with her husband's newfound reputation stood by him. Royce went on to make a second fortune, mainly in coastal property development.

Their collection of gold artefacts grew until decimated by a major robbery from their beach bach. The police advised them not to expect recovery as the artefacts, weighing approximately 40kg and valued in excess of $2,300,000, were now almost certainly gold bars.

No arrests have been made and the police say they have no leads.

◆　◆　◆

Rant and Rave

"Women!" I spat. "Can't live with 'em and can't live without them."

"Jesus, Rant." My mate Steve slopped his beer adding to the patina on the once pristine wood of the bar at the Anchors Aweigh.

"What are you on about now?"

My name isn't really Rant; it's Simon. My mates call me Rant because they reckon I lose my rag at the slightest provocation. I actually prefer Rant. A pansy name like Simon wouldn't go down well at the tyre shop where I'm the gun fitter. Man's work needs a man's name. I try and keep my temper in check at work; doesn't go down too well with the customers, not to mention Jake the owner.

After a hard day spinning up wheels and giving girls the eye I like to call in at the AA for a quick cold one that nearly always turns into lots of slow ones, especially if Steve is propping up the bar, which he usually is.

"Here I am slogging me guts out trying to make a dollar and my bloody girlfriend, oh pardon me, '*partner*' spends it as fast as I earn it," I went on. "Rave can't keep her hands off the plastic. The bitch is a spendthrift."

"Bloody hell, mate. You've only been living with her for how long?"

Steve wiped the froth from his moustache.

"You reckoned she was '*the one*' when you first shacked up a couple of months ago."

"Yeah. She *was* the one. But I've found out she can't keep her hands in her pockets; they're always in mine."

"I thought that's what having a partner was all about - sharing stuff."

Steve squeezed the beer out of his sodden shirt cuff.

My girlfriend's - pardon, *partner's* - name, Rave really is Rave, as in raving beauty. And she was…. is, I mean. Only now I don't seem to notice. What is it with girlfriends anyway? When did they elevate themselves to partners? What's become of partners, you know, the real kind, business partners or wives even? As soon as they elevate themselves from girlfriend to partner they start whining about this, that and the other. Worse, they start assuming they have rights like presuming they can make decisions without you.

As for business partners, unless I'm at a party or social function, not often right now, I admit, but could happen again when I get my own tyre shop, you have to introduce them as your *business partner* to show you aren't sleeping with them. Unless you are, when you have to pretend to deny it with a ridiculous chuckle.

Then the person you're introducing your partner to is probably thinking, 'Why aren't you rooting your partner? Is she a dog? Are you a dog? I don't want to do business with dogs.'

On the other hand if you don't do the denial chuckle he's saying to himself, 'You dirty dogs! I'm not doing business with you. You'll be too busy on your joint account instead of mine.'

I won't even go there if your partner is the same sex. Mind you, that's fashionable these days too. I see plenty of them coming in to have their tyres rotated. Makes me wild how they ponce around trying to catch my eye. If there's anything I can't stand it's gays. And when did they become gays, the sad bastards. Whatever happened to queers and homos?

"Take it easy, Rant," soothed Steve. "You'll bust your gut carrying on about shirt-lifters."

"OK, OK, you're right, Steve." I snapped out of it. "I digress big time; bad habit. Back to Rave. She's a flaming spendthrift. I wish she was my *business partner* then I could fire her."

"Give it a rest, mate."

Steve spluttered into his freshly-filled tankard thereby blowing froth on the dress of the woman sitting next to him.

"Hey!" I laughed. "That sheila hasn't even noticed you've spilled your head. Now that's the sort of girlfriend I need."

"Whaddaya mean? The uncomplaining sort or the sort that doesn't mind a bit of the amber down her back?"

Steve took a long draught before he thumped his tankard on the bar to indicate it was empty yet again.

"My round, mate," I said.

Hopefully Steve was too pissed to notice he was buying three rounds to my one.

"About time, you mingy bastard. You're three rounds behind. Only a bloody tightwad like you would think a gorgeous bint like Rave is an extravagant tart."

I returned with our cold ones determined to make Steve understand I was the aggrieved party here.

"Every bloody day I find Visa slips tucked away behind cushions or in drawers or half-pie hidden elsewhere. Mostly the slips are for what I'd call junk, but Rave seems to think we can't live without a 55-inch flat screen or electric matching tooth brushes or new clothes in case we get invited to someone's wedding. Our cards, pardon me, *my cards* are more than maxed; they're melted."

"Ever thought of spending a little less on yourself and a bit more time with her?"

All of a sudden Steve sounded sensible and sober.

"What! Why should I?" I was definitely aggrieved. "Look, mate, every time I find a stack of receipts we have a stand up. I rant and she raves. Plates fly around like Frisbees and things get broken. Sometimes that same vital appliance we couldn't live without."

Time to go home. Steve was ogling the women at the next table whose dress had nearly dried.

"Can I buy you a drink?" he asked.

"Oh, no," she said firmly. "My shout."

Steve always was a lucky bugger.

♦

When I got home to the flat Rave was sitting in a brand new vibrating lazy-boy massaging armchair. Worse, it was one of a matching pair arranged to take maximum advantage of the 55-five inch that had, until now, dominated the poxy little area the landlord had indicated was the lounge.

I'm not too sorry to say I lived up to my name and hit the roof. Literally, because it's so blimmen low. I got Rave in a headlock and forcibly removed the card from her person and cut it in two in front of her.

She wept and screamed. "You heartless bastard."

"I don't care," I told her. "It's for your own good and if you don't like it bugger off and *partner* up with some other chuckle-sucker."

Then I left her to stew while I went out to the carport the landlord likes to call the garage. There I lost myself in further work to restore my beautiful Holden V8. As I calmed down I mused about where Steve and I would go fishing at the weekend in my new sports fisher boat.

Girlfriends, women, partners ... Whatever. You can keep them.

No bloody idea how to save money.

Not a flamin' clue.

♦ ♦ ♦

Sailing Solo

In the time it took for me to slip, topple through the railing, snapping it as I went and splash into the sea I was able to panic, curse my own stupidity for not clipping on my life-line, worry the water would be too cold and panic again.

The shock of the water dispelled in an instant any hope it wasn't too cold - and also dispelled my panic.

I took stock. I was in the water, out of sight of land. My flotation vest had inflated. Good job I was wearing that. The sea was cold, either not as cold as at first or I was already numb.

There was a big swell, but the sea was calm with only about a five knot wind blowing. That's why I'd put up the spinnaker and set the self-steering with the boat nicely balanced. That same spinnaker was now taking Ragdoll away from me. Even now I had to wait for a swell to bear me up high enough so I could see the deck. I could see and hear my old dog still barking in my direction as if she wanted to jump in and be part of my game. I willed her not to.

Within minutes all I could see, even as I crested a swell, was the top of the mast and sails with the spinnaker drawing nicely. Meg's barking faded into silence. The sea was silent. There were no seabirds.

The silence overwhelmed me. It didn't seem possible that the big open ocean swells could move vast amounts of water without making a sound. They seemed malevolent in their silence.

I shouted, swore, cursed. When I ran out of noise it made the silence worse, frightening even. I lay back; let the flotation vest take my weight like an armchair. I didn't care to think about the unfathomable depth of water beneath me or what might be swimming in it. I dismissed thoughts of land. It had dropped below the horizon yesterday afternoon. My last dial up on the GPS put me twenty-four nautical miles off East Cape.

There was always a chance a fishing boat might be this far out and investigate a seemingly crewless yacht. Clutching at straws.

Maybe someone would call me up on the radio and raise the alarm when I didn't reply. Maybe, but that wouldn't happen for at least 24 hours. I cursed myself for thinking I could still sail single-handed at my age, even though I'd been doing it for years. I was stuffed. Unless a miracle occurred.

I yelled obscenities again, blaspheming the relentless swells. The silence absorbed my yells; made them puny. My anger dissipated, fading into self pity as tears welled adding infinitesimally to the ocean's volume.

What a miserable way to die. If I was going to die I resolved that I wasn't going to do so snivelling, feeling sorry for myself. Who would witness that? I didn't believe in God though right now it might have been helpful if I had. I intended a wry smile, but I doubt it made it to my face stiff with salt. So no divine intervention likely.

After how long in the water - thirty minutes, maybe - my watch was lost when I fell in - I realised I *was* going to die. As long as my flotation vest kept me afloat I wouldn't drown; but exposure, hypothermia, thirst or shark attack would finish me off surely enough. Yeah, there was that guy who survived in the water for days in Cook Straight a couple of years ago, but he was a trained survival expert diver in a wetsuit. Still, anything's possible.

Everyone is going to die. You could say we're starting to die once we stop growing when we're teenagers. Or, if you want to be morbid about it; we start dying the day we're born. I was going early, that's all. Thinking of death like that calmed me a little. And I was comfortable; the sea carried me along, rising and falling, surface barely ruffled, and a light wind kept me cool under a sun shielded by wispy clouds from being too fierce.

I *did* make an effort not to consider the future. Without conscious decision I found myself thinking of the past. The job I would never return to. I didn't like the jolt this gave me. I thought of the people in my life. My daughter due to graduate at the end of the year. Sitting her last papers now following a family tradition to be a pharmacist.

Why didn't we have more than one child, I mused? Probably because I split with her mother, my first wife. She had an affair and I took umbrage. How stupid of me. Call it guilt disguised as umbrage. Oh, I didn't exactly cheat on her, but I surely thought about it a few times.

Chance would have been a fine thing.

I wish I'd been a bit more grown up about it; seen her straying for what it was with the benefit of hindsight, a cry for attention. But the shop was going through a growth phase right then. I had to put in the hours.

I realised I'd been voicing these thoughts out loud to the silent witness of the sea as I rose and fell with the gentle giant swells. My eyes closed involuntarily against the glare and the occasional salty wavelet slapped my face. When the next swell bore me effortlessly up I swept the horizon. I expected nothing, hoped for something.

Expectations met, hopes dashed once more. I sighed, choked back a sob and retreated into my thoughts again.

The pity of it was that my second marriage was not so much a disaster as uncomfortable. Started off brilliantly. Romantic and touchy-feely yet after only a short while, something was missing. Trust, maybe. I couldn't help wondering sometimes if this annoying habit or that irritating mannerism was the final straw that ended her first marriage.

Then I couldn't help wondering if she thought that of me.

I know my daughter, almost a teenager, never quite connected with her stepmother. She soon found excuses to not spend time with us. I regretted that, but couldn't see how to resolve the situation so let it drift. How sad and how stupid of me.

For all that I've been seeing much more of my daughter since she started at uni. I was thrilled when she took up pharmacology. She comes into the shop a lot now and works with me full time between semesters.

I drifted into thinking about my parents, married for sixty years with not a cross word between them. They died within months of each other; Dad first then Mum, almost certainly of a broken heart.

Although she seemed cheerful enough it was as if she didn't want to live without him.

Strange how their example of loving stability, broadcast wide at every significant anniversary, was not followed by their children. Like me, neither my brother or sister could sustain their marriages. I know how this hurt and puzzled them.

It's obvious, too late for me, that when you love someone you have to put them before your own selfish agenda. When you first fall in love you do this anyway. Then lust cools and life gets in the way. But you made the commitment so you must carry on and put her first. After a while, a very short while, that selflessness becomes ingrained and trust endures. Before you realise it a deeper, enduring love develops. Wouldn't you know it, that deeper love conjures up lust, occasionally, time and circumstance permitting.

'Now you tell me,' I mouthed to the heavens where the god I didn't believe in allegedly resided. Descending to the depths seemed a much more likely outcome than ascending upwards.

I was raving. Better than the alternative. You're a long time dead and the ocean floor was a long way down.

I wondered who 'you' was. Maybe I *had* found 'God.' Maybe 'you' was 'God.' It came to me that this is how we face death; by retreating into ourselves. Thinking about the good things, the precious moments. Yet how insignificant each is in the greater scheme of things. I laughed out loud as I realised I had attributed life to a 'greater scheme'. I, who had been an atheist and believer in the logic of evolution all my adult years, succumbing as I neared the pearly gates to the hocus-pocus of religion.

My laughter startled me back to awareness of my desperate situation. I couldn't feel any of my extremities now. Not that the water was freezing, but even at summer temperatures the cold had worked into my body, now almost totally immersed.

The sun was dipping below the horizon, a little more each time I rose to the summit of a swell. I calculated I must have been in the water over seven hours. Soon it would be fully dark. I doubted I would survive the night.

I watched the sun set for as long as I could. As I was borne up on a convenient swell I saw for the first time of watching countless sunsets the green flash as it dipped. I felt an extraordinary gratitude to the ocean for allowing me that last green glimpse. I started to cry with self pity; mortification at all things lost and all that might have been.

I pulled myself together determined not to drown in self-pity. Very funny. I am going to drown, only not in self pity. I began to sing as best I could. Springsteen's 'Glory Days.' Gerry Rafferty's 'Get It Right Next Time' followed by 'Stuck in the Middle With You.' Oh yeah I was hilarious.

The effort of singing exhausted me, and the occasional mouthful of cold seawater made it a little difficult. I relapsed again into musing and must have drifted off to sleep as the sky darkened. I dreamt I was holding my daughter on my knee when she was a little girl with my first wife busily setting out a picnic on a grassy bank next to a small clear creek. My wife looked fondly at us as I bounced my daughter up and down. The up and down became insistent until the vision faded to be replaced by the grim reality that the bouncing was waves buffeting me as the wind got up.

Just a moment. The wind hadn't got up; it had dropped if anything. Something was causing the rough water. I kicked and trod water, calm acceptance of death forgotten. In fear I swivelled around, expecting orcas or sharks.

I stared in shock. I must still be dreaming. A slight hum like a vibration coming through the water confirmed what I saw, rising like a whale from the deep. A submarine. Even though it was dark I could clearly see it was a sub sitting there impervious to the swell. Long, low on the water, black steel glistening in the moonlight, still wet from the sea from which it had emerged.

"It's a miracle," I shouted. "There is a God."

Immediately I felt foolish at attributing divine intervention to my rescue, after so recently eschewing its existence as part of my near demise.

With what seemed to me extraordinary efficiency the crew silently hauled me aboard and bustled me below, cleaned me up, fed me and clothed me in navy fatigues.

"Welcome aboard, bud."

The man who appeared to be in charge didn't look old enough, but the badge pinned to his shirt said 'Captain, US Navy.'

Still woozy from my ordeal and completely taken aback at my good fortune I said to the boy-captain, "What are you doing here off New Zealand's coast?"

"Waaal, I guess it won't make no odds to tell you," he drawled. "Since a couple of your sandal wearing tree huggers stabbed our why-hope-eye spy station to death we've had a nuclear sub on-station filling in the communication gap."

I absorbed this bombshell while appreciating his apt pronunciation of Waihopai.

"Is our government aware of this?"

"Sure thing, pal, that's why we picked you up. You were drifting back into Kiwi territorial waters. We'd been watching you for some time, it was either save you now or let you die later inside the twelve mile limit. We are under strict orders to stay outside the twelve mile which we do…ah…mostly."

"So what now? My people will be worried. Can you drop me at Gisborne?"

"Fraid not, buddy."

Now the Captain was all business he didn't seem so young.

"In cases like this your government and ours has decreed that for our countries' mutual security in our war on terror we detain you on board until we can deliver you to authorities who will provide you with lifelong accommodation and sustenance in a secure and secret location in continental USA."

"You mean to all intents and purposes I'm a dead man because the politicians say so?"

I was appalled.

"You got it. But you would have been dead anyway if we hadn't come along. I can assure you there were no other vessels likely to rescue you."

"What about my yacht and dog? Can't you catch up with them and put me on board. I won't say anything about this. Nobody would believe me anyway."

"Ah, well." The Captain looked sheepish. "We've used your yacht as an exercise, sent it to the bottom with one of our new underwater sonar guided torpedoes. I'm afraid your dog is a casualty of our war on terror."

"You're kidding me! My old dog was a terrorist threat to the USA?"

"Look on the upside, pal, I've heard the secure facility where you'll be going is like my idea of heaven; golf course, pool, bars, bowling alley, movies, cable, fast food of all kinds and even women and you can probably have another dog there for all I know. Better than any old folks home you might have ended up in. Think about it, you're just going a little early, is all."

I did think about it. I wasn't at all sure I'd been 'saved' after all.

◆　◆　◆

Falling Out

I was sitting at my desk on the seventy-fifth floor of the South Tower of the World Trade Center staring unseeing out of the floor to ceiling window of my corner office. Instead of the skyscrapers of Manhattan and the sweep of Hudson Bay I saw through my wide open eyes myself running along a beach with my mother and father on either side holding on to my hands and swinging me along. We splashed gleefully through the sea as it swirled up around us before rushing out again. I came to the appalling conclusion that that day nearly twenty-five years ago was the last day of real unadulterated happiness I had enjoyed.

Shortly after that day my parents divorced and I began a life of puzzlement and insecurity, of being shuffled to and fro for reasons I couldn't fathom. Yeah, I grew up with something to prove all right. After they split I stayed with my father who, as far as I was concerned, didn't give much of a good god-damn about me. It was only my good Jewish aunts and uncles who kept me from being the complete arsehole and fired me up with the ambition to get even. With whom or what I couldn't say but sticking it up the Arabs seemed a good enough generic revenge motive in the absence of anything more personal. After all, everyone else had it in for those sand-surfers.

Only this morning had I found out the true reason my parents divorced. A birthday card from my Aunt Rachel arrived, two weeks late and for my thirty-fifth when it was actually my thirty-sixth, but hey it's the thought that counts. Not that I credit my aunt with much ability to think of anyone but herself. She had included a chatty letter mentioning Ermanno had won a television dance contest in Italy and my mother had been seen with him leaving the studio. Dopey old Aunt Rachel had forgotten I had never been told the circumstances of my mother's abrupt disappearance.

So it wasn't, as I'd been led to believe, the banal 'mummy/daddy doesn't love mummy/daddy anymore' bullshit. Apparently, my mother had run off with her dancing instructor. And he was a frigging Eye-talian to boot! No doubt like all those greasy lounge-lurkers he was better at the horizontal rumba than my father.

Dismissing the unsavoury picture of my parents having sex I sat there staring blindly at the view thinking about my shitty life.

To be honest my life wasn't too shitty given my shaky start. At thirty-six I was the youngest high limit oil futures trader at Stein, Weisberg and Streisand or SWS as it was known. We specialised in shafting the Arabs by buying long and selling short. Needless to say SWS had had a few death threats made against them, but usually to our offices in Tel Aviv or London, never here in New York. So far.

I didn't have time for a social life nor did I want one. That's what I told myself anyway. To tell the truth social life didn't want me. Girls, women, whatever we're supposed to call them now, didn't stay with me for long. The bitches invariably took off into the wild blue yonder right after I'd lavished some expensive gift on them. The trouble with Jewish girls is they're all gold-diggers.

To be fair I've become paranoid about letting anyone into my life. SWS's competitors and even the OPEC countries we specialise in are capable of industrial espionage. Kind of why I have to limit myself to dating Jewish ladies.

I might have made a mistake with the latest. Sarah's by far the most beautiful of the women I've dated lately. Taller than me even with her stilettos kicked off, legs all the way up, although I've yet to find out how far 'up' is. An hour glass figure and a face to die for with no hint of the usual Jewish moustache. Her silky black hair hangs almost to the small of her back.

She says Jewish; but I found a letter return address Tehran, Iran in her handbag which she had uncharacteristically left on my coffee table when she went to the bathroom. Her name was spelt the Arabic way, Sara, which like the return address could mean something or nothing.

She says: tanned from holidaying in the Med with her last boyfriend. I now suspect permanent pigmentation from birth. Again I've not yet been able to confirm that. Somehow at the last

149

moment Sarah wiggles out of disporting herself in my bed. So far she has refused my blandishments, even eschewing the keys of a new Cadillac I offered her.

Despite my misgivings she's like an addictive drug to me and if it wasn't for that I would have blown her off by now. As it is she is a distraction just when I need to keep my eye on the ball as oil prices respond to unrest in the Middle-East.

To keep ahead of the futures game I needed to stay focused exclusively on the job. The hours were long and the risks enormous, although, to be honest, I usually managed to lay the risk off on someone else. I enjoyed the notoriety of being the hardest, fastest trader. I was the comer who, one day soon, would surely achieve more than in-company fame; something I had been craving all my life. Not that there was anything to sneeze about where in-company fame was concerned because it was usually accompanied by company largesse.

In fact later that very afternoon, in front of all the other envious traders who hated me to a man, I was due to receive a commendation from the C.E.O. for pulling off the largest margin call in the company's history that would seriously make a dent in the GDP of a few of those towel-head sandpits. The commendation should have at least six fat, round zeros lined up behind whatever prime number on the check the boss decided was appropriate enough to tuck into my silk lined pocket.

As I gazed out the window wishing the commendation was over and I could hightail it out to the Hamptons where Sarah waited and money counted I noticed the glint of sun on wings as an aircraft turned towards Manhattan. I thought nothing of it as passed away to the north out of my sight. Shortly thereafter I felt the building shake as though from a violent wind gust and indeed thought that is what it was. The lights flickered momentarily then came back on. I peered over the partition that delineated my office in the open plan room. Everybody settled back down to their phones and computer screens as though nothing had happened.

But I knew better or more accurately; worse. I could see smoke drifting up past the window. This was the first time I'd noticed smoke; at this height there shouldn't have been any. I got up from my desk and by pressing my face against the sealed glass I could see flames shooting out the North Tower near the top floors.

I looked at my Cartier to check if I'd been at my desk long enough to justify logging off to grab a coffee. I saw it was barely nine, which meant as I'd been hard at it since seven a break would be acceptable. Maybe by the time I'd got to the canteen the fire in the North Tower would be breaking news.

Before I'd made it half way across the trading floor past gnome-like figures hunched over flickering computer screens, which, it occurred to me, is how I must look when in full killer mode, there was a loud kerumph and a violent shake. This was much worse than before.

Someone who must have disobeyed company orders by surfing onto a news site screamed out, 'We've been hit by a plane. Same as the North Tower.' My initial thought that the North Tower must have had some sort of gas explosion evaporated. I rushed back to my corner and peered down because it felt like the hit was lower than the damage on the North Tower.

I could make out smoke and flame billowing out from a huge hole some fifteen floors below. At that moment pandemonium erupted, the lights went out and stayed out, acrid smoke invaded the room through every air-conditioning vent, and suddenly it got very hot. People started screaming.

With what I had seen out the window I knew the only hope lay in retreating upwards. Keeping more or less calm I pushed my way to the emergency stairs and began climbing up to the higher floors. I have to say that I was grateful for the hours I'd spent in the gym as I elbowed the sedentary aside.

To my horror the fire seemed to be gaining so that by the time I got to the eighty-second floor the heat was intense, but worse, the building vibrated now and again. The lurching didn't feel right at all.

151

Those who could climbed higher. The obese, unfortunately the majority, gave up and sat on the steps or found an empty chair on whatever floor they were passing, convinced the fire would be extinguished. I didn't disabuse them of that notion. I had seen the fire and knew that the fewer of us who made it to the top the more likely it was that I personally would be rescued. Maybe there was some sort of observation platform from which a helicopter could pluck a few of us to safety.

Shortly after I got to the ninety-eighth floor, with only another ten to go while I sat and caught my breath, the building gave a definite lurch to the left, seeming to drop a few feet like an aircraft in turbulence then swayed back to the right. I stood up and went to the nearest window and looked out, as I had done a lifetime ago though less than an hour had passed.

The clocks festooning the walls indicated this floor was a trading room of sorts like the one I'd recently spent more hours in than my apartment. The clocks showed the time in London, Moscow, Paris, Sidney, Hong Kong, Dubai, Riyadh, Baghdad, Tel Aviv; anywhere important in the world. It was strange to think that while I was here stuck like a rat in a trap other people there were going about their daily lives.

I looked down the vertical drop to the streets below. Amazingly it looked as though the people of New York were as unconcerned as those people in far away cities about what was happening up here to me on the ninety-eighth floor. I could see people smaller than ants scurrying about, cars and buses like tiny toys moving slowly up and down streets. Look up, please look up, save me please, I silently implored them.

The next lurch made the glass of the window shatter; in fact all the windows shattered and in so doing all hell broke loose. The noise of the inferno increased tenfold. The calm silence inside the building was abruptly replaced by the roar of the inrushing wind as it fed the flames. Paper and the paraphernalia of office life swirled about.

The next second I felt again the dropping sensation of a plane in turbulence. This time it didn't stop for at least thirty long seconds. I reasoned the building must be doomed. I needed to get to the observation platform so I started climbing again. Before I had even made it to the stairway door the floor tilted and I was sliding across the floor and heading straight for a glassless window.

As I passed a tangle of office furniture survival instinct kicked in and I grabbed a chair, screaming in terror as I exited the building hanging on to it. Then it jammed crosswise in the frame. I screamed again with relief. Desks and chairs, computers and photocopiers cascaded past me into the void.

At that moment my cell went off with its rendition of the opening bars of Rocky's Eye of the Tiger. Salvation. Someone was on the way to help. I had no idea how I could be rescued dangling in space, totally reliant on the strength of a flimsy aluminium chair most likely made in China. But that wasn't my problem.

I fished out my phone with my free hand and thumbed up the text message. 'GOTCHA,' it said, 'May you rot in hell, Sara, without an 'h.'

The cheap chair folded in on itself.

Yes, I was the 'Falling Man', famous even if only for the fifteen seconds it took me to plummet ninety-eight floors. Still, it was fame of a sort, however brief. No doubt the media would digitally erase me from news reports for fear of upsetting people.

The pity of it all, I mused as the streets of Manhattan zoomed towards me like the opening sequence of a movie, is that everybody would think the attacks the work of Muslim terrorists. I knew better, I always did.

It was the work of a vindictive woman who held no personal grudge. She disliked all Jews. I couldn't accept it was me she disliked.

The Caddy must have been a mistake. If only I'd offered her a Lambo or a Ferrari.

◆　◆　◆

153

Sweet Gail

"What the bloody hell do you think you're doing?"

"Well," Gail drawls, turning around slowly. She lets the dressing-gown she'd borrowed from her boyfriend Brian fall open.

"Just having a little look round, Nev. Didn't think you'd mind. Brian said you wouldn't be back for hours."

Neville, drunkenly deflated by the girl's insolent attitude and simultaneously aroused by the glimpse of her nakedness, slurs, "That kid knows fuck all. Bet he doesn't know you're parading around my house like the slut you are."

"No need to be nasty, Nev. I can be very, *very* nice when it suits."

Gail half-steps back as the overweight, sweating Neville lurches towards her, groping at her gown. His comb-over fails to disguise his balding head.

"Yeah? How about being nice right now then? Come to my room. My bed's twice as big and I'm twice the man my wimpy son is. Don't know what you see in that soft bugger anyway."

"Now, now, Nev. None of that," Gail replies, sweetly insincere. "What would Brian say?"

She lets Neville think he has her as he wraps his stubby arms around her waist. Just as he reaches to rip off the robe, she brings up her knee with considerable speed and force and gets him right in the balls. As he releases her and doubles over in agony she lightly slaps him across the face.

"I said no and I meant no," she says evenly. "Wait 'til I tell Brian what a sleazebag you are."

"Ow, Christ, you fucking bitch." Neville clutches his nether region. "You wouldn't dare tell him. I'll tell him you led me on, prancing around with no clothes on."

"You're drunk. You're imagining things." Gail barely raises her voice. "Why would I lead on a loser like you? Brian will never believe you. He knows what you're like. I'm going to dob you in right now."

Threatened tears could be a residual from the recent assault on his privates.

"Please, Gail," Neville whines. "Don't. I've fucked up everything else. Brian's the only family I've got left."

◆

Gail leaves the snivelling drunk sprawled, legs splayed, on the living room floor as she retraces her steps to the bedroom. She likes the half light provided by the street lamps; not that she needs light to find her way around. She'd been through the house plenty of times before. Her mental inventory of everything is comprehensive.

She catches sight of herself as she passes a full length mirror in the hall and is taken as usual with herself and her partial Goth style. She fingers the piercings in her eyebrow and gently flicks the ring through her lip with her tongue so that it glitters in the gloom. She draws back the gown to reveal her white skin and the bird tattoos that adorn her stomach. She admires how the brilliant reds and greens of the parrot contrast with her black hair.

Her eyes lose focus as she admits inwardly that she is envious of the wealth the house represents since property values spiralled upward. She knows she hasn't got a show of ever owning a house like this or any other, even a rundown ex-statey in South Auckland. Yet true to her Goth values she can't help being a bit contemptuous of the ponderous sixties brick and tile house that screams boring suburban.

Gail pauses to check on her dozy boyfriend's still-sleeping form. Brian hasn't got a hope of buying a house either. Why is she even with him? Careful not to wake him she shrugs off the gown and climbs into his bed.

◆

"Don't rub too hard," calls Brian to his father who is cleaning his classic Holden on the drive. "You might polish right through."

Neville's sunnies hide his hangover and his expression.

"Morning, son." He is unusually amiable. "She's a beauty, isn't she? Hope I didn't wake you last night. Everything all right? How's your girlfriend this morning?"

Brian saunters out, yawning and stretching. Idly he scratches his balls through his cotton pajama shorts. He fails to notice his father wince. Brian leans on the gleaming paintwork.

"Yeah, sweet. Why wouldn't it be?" he replies nonchalantly. "Hey, Nev, you've missed a spot."

He rubs an imaginary blemish to rark up the old man.

"Get your bloody mitts off there, boyo, unless you want a clip around the ear!" Neville growls. "Now I asked, how's your girlfriend this morning?"

"I've already told you; everything's sweet. What's it to you anyway?"

"Nothing, sweet eff all. It's just I've been thinking about you and that girlfriend of yours. I dunno what you see in a Goth bitch like her. She's a bad influence, her and that crowd of hoons you hang out with. Take it from me, they're trouble and that's where you'll land any time soon. Anyway, it's not right you sleeping with her in my house. If your mother was here she wouldn't allow it."

"You've gotta be dreaming Nev. Mum couldn't have cared less. She was having it off with that slimy dance teacher way before she walked out on you. My friends are my business so keep your nose out of it."

Right on time to catch Brian's last sentence Gail comes out of the house. She's back in the robe and she too yawns and stretches to unashamedly reveal herself to father and son.

"Yay! You tell him, Bri. And that's not the only thing he should keep his nose out of."

"What do you mean, doll?"

Gail flings an arch look at Neville. Neville looks away though beneath his sunglasses he couldn't stop his eyes swivelling down.

He is drawn by lust back to the slut even as he marvels inwardly that a solid Kiwi bloke like him could possibly hanker for a Goth bitch like Gail.

"Tell you later, Bri."

Gail smirks at Neville and lets the silk fall open. Let him enjoy his stolen eyeful. "Come on let's go back inside and have some fun."

♦

The sound effects from Grand Theft Auto blank out all external noise from Brian's bedroom as he and Gail battle it out for gang supremacy in the virtual American cityscape. Gail panders to Brian's ego by throwing a stage. She submits to his advances for a few minutes then pulls away.

"Your old man. Loaded, is he, Bri?"

"Yeah, suppose so. He forks out for me anyway, pays my fines and that. He's not a bad arsehole, even if he does think more of his crappy old cars than me."

Eager to resume where he left off, Brian buries his face between Gail's breasts.

Gail pushes him away.

"Yeah, but what about your Mum? Doesn't he cough up for her?"

"Nah. She ran off with a rich dance teacher dude. Richer than Dad. Said she wouldn't take his dough as long as he saw me right."

The front door slams as Neville comes back into the house. Over the endless looping racket of the video game they barely catch his shouts.

"I'm off out, Brian. Going to the pub with Mitch. Lock up if you go out and don't drink and drive. Don't forget, the cops know your car."

"Yeah, OK," Brian yells, adding quietly to Gail, "Bossy old bugger."

"Neat. We've got the house to ourselves." Gail bounces up and down on the bed with glee. "Let's get stuck in to your old man's vodka. Want one?"

"Hang on, doll. My cell phone's demanding attention." He studies it. "Spider and the guys. They want to meet up later, see if we can't scrub off a few more tyres."

"OK, but let's have a drink first." Gail pouts. "Fetch me a double from your Dad's liquor and I'll let you do what you were doing before."

She pushes his hand away as he fingers her left nipple. "And pinch his grass while you're about it."

Brian is doubtful.

"He'll give me a slapping if he finds out. The vodka I can water down, but he'll notice the grass is missing."

"What do you care? Slap him back. Show him who's boss."

When Brian returns he lights up the spliff and passes it to Gail. They take long pulls on the vodka in turn until they're laughing and giggling, at what neither could say. As Brian begins to make progress with Gail, now flat on her back on the bed, she sits up.

"I've got a great idea! Let's take your father's Holden and meet up with Spider," she urges, excited. "We'll have it back before he comes home. Anyway he'll be so pissed he won't notice even if he comes back before us."

"I dunno, Gail." Her suggestion sobers Brian. "You know how much he thinks of that old heap."

"Aw, come on, Bri. Don't be a wimp." She winds her arms around him, presses her body close. "Time you stood up to the dirty bugger. Show him he can't have everything his way all the time. Besides it's only an old '72 HQ, common as, hardly the classic your old man thinks it is."

She bends close and whispers in his ear, "I know where he hides the keys."

◆

Spider and his street racing gang are gathered under the street lights of a new and as yet unoccupied housing development when Brian and Gail roll up in the Holden. They crowd around and poke fun at the car so different from their tricked up, lowered, boy racer rice burner types. Secretly they can't help admiring the Holden's pristine condition.

"Go on, Bri, show them what she can do."

Brian executes a few perfect doughnuts. Tyre smoke pours off the rear tyres like a fuely dragster at the strip. Spider, Gail, boy racers and girlfriends whoop and holler, egging Brian on until he comes to a sliding halt amidst a cloud of smoke and catcalls from the crowd.

♦

Neville sprawls across the passenger seat of his mate's ute. He never takes his Holden when he and Mitch are on the binge.

"Bloody good night, eh, Mitch? Good job you're driving. Didn't mean to get this pissed so quick."

He sits up when they come to the lights at the intersection that leads to the new subdivision. Mitch almost stops for the red but cruises on through as Neville reaches across in front of him pointing out the driver's window.

"Hey, look at that lot of bloody hoons. Bet my bloody son is in there somewhere. Christ! That looks like my bloody Holden. The little prick's stolen my bloody car. Quick, pull over, mate. I'm gonna sort out that little shit."

♦

"Who's this then, Brian?" Spider asks as Neville marches up to the gathered youths.

"Fuck off, you old bugger," calls another.

"Yeah, fuck off, you old fart."

A chorus from others rendered bold by the group.

159

"Shit!" groans Brian. "It's my old man."

"You're for it now, Brian." Gail laughs wickedly. "Told you we shouldn't take your father's pride and joy."

Brian gapes in disbelief. Is she joking or telling an outright lie?

Neville shouts to make himself heard above the catcalls and ignores the threatening youths who close in around him.

"What the bloody hell do you think you're doing, Brian?"

"Keep your shirt on, Nev. Just having a bit of fun. Anyway Gail wanted to see how your old heap went."

Brian reckons he has nothing to lose dropping Gail in it.

"Yeah, that's right, Nev," Gail shouts, unfazed by Brian's cowardice. "I wanted to see how the old heap went."

She gestures obscenely and the crowd roar in appreciation and chant, "Come on, NEV. Show us how the old heap goes!"

"Go on then, Nev," Gail taunts, "if you think you've got the balls for it!"

Neville hesitates then shoulders through the mob and clambers into his Holden. They cheer and clap as he attempts to do a doughnut, ragged in comparison with the smooth display Brian gave earlier. Sensing they're in control and can smell blood, the hoons urge him on to do another looping, tyre-squealing doughnut.

In a manic trance he spins the car into a series of circles. The motor screams. Each loop gets wilder until the car clips the curb and spins out of control and flips on its roof. The Holden slides along showering sparks like an inverted flaming meteor.

The crowd is deathly silent for an instant, then surge forward with whoops and howls. As they near the upturned wreck dripping petrol ignites on the red hot exhaust. In a millisecond like a flaming ball the car erupts

Brian and Gail stand disbelieving and stunned and then, as sirens sound in the distance, turn as one with the mob and race for their cars. Spider pulls them both into his car and accelerates away from the scene, tyres smoking, cursing mates who get in his way.

♦

"Fucking hell! Did you see that? We should have stopped him making a fool of himself. Christ! We should have helped the silly bugger."

White-faced with shock, Brian twists in his seat to glimpse the funeral pyre that is his father's.

"Forget it, *Bri!* He might have been your old man but he didn't give a shit about you." Gail recovers her cool. "He cared more about his stupid car."

"Yeah, you're right. But what about the cops?" whines Brian. "They'll suss out whose car it was pretty quick."

"So what, you wimp? Spider'll drop us off at your old man's place in a minute and we'll just say we've been there all night." Gail studies her nails as though without a care in the world. "Look, you said yourself Nev was always a big-headed loser. Let's get on the piss when we get home."

Brian recovers his colour as he considers his cool Goth girlfriend. A little doubtful, he says nothing.

♦

Gail reclines on the big double bed that was recently Neville's.

"Make mine a treble," she calls out to Brian. He is in the lounge rifling through the bottles in the drinks cabinet.

"OK, doll."

Already well over the shock of seeing his father go up in smoke.

Gail gazes at herself in the antique mirror that Nev had placed at the end of the bed for reasons she can well imagine. She admires her pale complexion, framed by black hair, and emphasised with purple lipstick and eye-shadow. She pouts and whispers, "The randy old bastard's wish came true. He got me into his bed."

Brian surprises her.

"Speak up, doll," he yells. "I can't hear you."

How could he hear her over the clinking of bottles?

Gail grimaces at her reflection and yells back, careful to sound sad.

"I said it's a real bummer your old man writing himself off like that. Still, I reckon he had it coming. S'pose you'll get the house and everything now eh, Bri?"

With a glass of amber liquid in each hand Brian comes back into the bedroom.

"Yeah, I reckon. Dunno what it's worth though."

"I do, lover boy. I'm … we're gonna be sweet. Hope you've made mine a treble. A girl's entitled."

♦   ♦   ♦

Waiouru, my Vietnam

"ATTEN-SHUN!" screamed Corporal Davis. Nobody moved. Tom Shepherd, birth date 14th March, slowly lowered the comic he had been reading, unfolded himself from his bed, stood up to his full height of six foot two, sauntered to where he stood towering over the Corporal, leaned over so that his nose and the Corporal's were almost touching and bellowed in his face, "FUCK OFF!"

Corporal Davis recoiled as though struck with the butt of the standard issue 7.62mm FN self loading rifle. Trying desperately to maintain his authority, he stammered, "Officer Cadet Shepherd, I will not be spoken to in that manner. I am going to put you on a charge!"

Tom said nothing. He reached out, encircled Corporal Davis's ramrod-straight figure in a bear hug and lifted him bodily off the floor.

"And I'm going to throw you out the window, Corporal Davis, unless you behave yourself."

The rest of us couldn't help it; we all started to laugh and taunt the Corporal.

"Yeah, Corp, we'll say you were on the turps and fell out. Come on, Corp, don't be an arsehole. We know you think this war is crap just like us."

And so on.

We got up from our beds or footlockers, wherever we'd been lolling, and circled around Tom and the suspended corporal. Like wolves around prey, we scented blood.

"Go on, chuck him out, Tommy."

"Give him a taste of his own medicine."

"Serve the little Hitler right."

The taunts came thick and fast. Corporal Davis might have been reasonably sure we were joking, but he couldn't fathom Tom.

The corporal could have salvaged some of his dignity if he had stuck to his guns. He made the mistake of snivelling.

"Come on, boys. I'm supposed to be in charge here. I'm only following orders, trying to do my job. You'll get me kicked out of the army if the Sergeant-Major finds out about this."

Tom dropped him. He fell to the floor like a sack of the spuds we had to peel when we were raw squaddies. Someone kicked him, not hard, just enough to let him know we all thought he was a sanctimonious turd, an annoying little prick, expecting us all to jump up to attention whenever he came into our barracks.

No one said a word. We all turned away, picked up our paperbacks, our letters or went back to playing cards, whatever we'd been doing before this sorry little drama played out.

No one looked up as Corporal Davis got up and slunk away to the cubicle that was his quarters at the far end of the barracks.

I looked around the room at the guys all now engrossed as though nothing had happened. A few months ago an incident like this would have been inconceivable. Insubordination meant a trip to the glasshouse; not a pleasant prospect in Waiouru's winter. Now, as hardened, experienced, soon-to-be officers, we didn't give a toss.

As officer cadets not yet quite outranking the Corporal I thought discretion might be the better part of valour. I leaned over to the next bed and said to Roger, birth date 9th April, "Hope the little Corp doesn't dob us in for insubordination."

Roger lowered the law book he'd been studying.

"Not a chance. He's too worried about his own skin to rock the boat now. Anyway we'll outrank him in a couple of days when we get our pips."

I thought about that for a moment then said, "You're probably right, but you never know with these regular army types. They only know how to go by the book and take orders. I'd better go and make sure he's on our wavelength."

The other eleven guys had been listening and I got up to a chorus of approval.

"Good on you, Jacko."

"Always the peacemaker, Jacko."

164

"Sort the little shit out, mate."

I gave them a wry salute, a parody of the kind we would soon be returning in earnest, as I made my way out of the barrack room to the Corporal's cubicle.

I knocked on his door. There was no answer. I put my ear the door. I could hear sobbing. I pushed the door not expecting it to open. As it swung I saw the Corporal hunched up on his bed, shoulders heaving as he blubbered.

Christ, I thought. The army is human after all, or at least this little part of it is.

In all our months of training we draftees had been extended no sign of humanity or compassion from regular force rank of any kind. In fact, most of the bastards had a sadistic streak, which they especially enjoyed inflicting on the soldiers in the Officer Cadet Training Unit. Now here was one of them bawling his eyes out. I didn't have it in me to feel sorry for the little prick.

"Come on, Corp, Tommy wouldn't have tossed you out. Even if he tried we would have stopped him. Honest."

I was far from certain it was the truth, but what the hell. I got no response.

"For fuck's sake, man, get a grip on yourself. It's not the end of the world. You're supposed to be in charge of us, at least until the day after tomorrow."

Corporal Davis looked up.

"I know." His face was sullen. "You and your smartarse mates are just pretending to be soldiers. This is my life, all that I'm good for. If the army finds out I'm a hopeless NCO and worse, don't like girls, they'll kick me out for sure."

I wasn't sure I'd heard right.

"What do you mean, 'don't like girls?' Every man and his dog in the army likes girls don't they?"

The Corporal didn't reply.

"You mean there's more to this than just me and the boys winding you up, having a bit of fun?"

"Yeah, it's not just that."

165

He sounded oddly detached.

"My boyfriend has been posted to Vietnam; he's leaving in two days."

"What do you mean, your boyfriend?" I said, incredulous. "Don't tell me you're a poofter?"

The Corporal didn't answer; confirming his statement by hanging his head. His shoulders heaved as he resumed sobbing, quietly desperate.

"Look, Corp, just play it cool for a couple more days. Me and the others won't say anything. What are your problems to us anyway? We'll obey your orders when anyone else is around to keep up appearances, as long as you don't boss us around too much."

I left him and went back to the barrack room. The others looked up and fell silent. I stared back just as silently at my brothers-in-arms whose birthdays were as unlucky as mine. Brothers who resented the unceremonious interruption to our lives, yanked from our mothers and fathers, girlfriends and jobs, homes, farms, towns and cities. Brothers who had endured days of running around in the deep, damp snow of the Ruapehu rainforest and the desert plains of Waiouru.

We had seen our number dwindle to the twelve of us left. Sunday after Sunday we had been compelled to sit through the Army's stupid lectures on 'Why We Are There' with a big red arrow pointing at Vietnam; explaining how the Yellow Peril was going to domino its way down Dominion Road to our suburbs to murder our mothers, rape our sisters and convert the rest of us to communism.

"Guys, I shouldn't be telling on the poor bastard, but I'm going to anyway. Our Corporal is a poof!"

I couldn't resist it. Revenge was too sweet; on the army, the government, the Yanks for getting us into this, the desk jockey who pulled out my birth date, 28th March. At that moment poor Corporal Davis had the misfortune to be all of those culprits.

Gleeful pandemonium broke out.

"I don't bloody believe it. The dirty little fucker. That's the bloody army for you. Who would have thought it?"

"What do you reckon, Jacko?" asked Mike, birth date 19th April. "How about we go and wind the little prick up some more?"

"Better not, guys," I said. "The poor sod is in a bad way. We've done enough, had our revenge. Anyway we'll be out of here soon so why should we care?"

"Good on you, Jacko," called Tom. "Keeping us out of trouble as usual."

We all settled down again. One last brief chance before lights out to finish letters, polish our boots or yak about girls and getting out back to civilian life.

♦

The report from an FN 7.62mm self loading rifle is awesome to hear outside; deafening inside. Designed to kill a man more than a mile away in the wide open spaces of desert warfare, unwieldy and unnecessary in the jungles of Vietnam but issued anyway, the SLR at close range had the hitting power of a cannon.

We rushed to the Corporal's cubicle. The door was blown off; so was his head. Blood and gore everywhere. He had removed a boot and triggered the thing with his toe. We stood, all of us stunned and staring. We might have thought we were pretty tough, but nothing had prepared us for this. Finally Tom spoke.

"The poor sod. If I'd known this was going to happen I'd never have told him to fuck off."

"Don't worry," I said, "It wasn't your fault. It wasn't that he was queer either. It was his boyfriend being sent to Vietnam that did it."

"Yeah, but we shouldn't have baited him," said Roger. "We should have gone along with the poor bugger."

"Well, he's not a poor bugger anymore," I said. "Look out, here come the cavalry!"

We could hear the pounding of boots as the MPs charged across the small parade ground that separated the officer cadets' quarters from the rest of the barracks. The door burst open and the Sergeant Major at the van of the posse of MPs glared at us.

"What the bloody hell is going on here, Officer Cadet Shepherd?"

By way of reply we all moved aside so that the Sergeant Major could see the gory mess. Tom at ramrod attention said, "Suicide, Sarn't Major!"

"Any of you so-called Officer Cadets know anything about this?"

"No, Sarn't Major!' we chorused, equally rigid.

"If you know what's good for you and the army you'd all better keep it that way or you won't be getting your pips."

As if we cared.

"Yes, Sarn't Major!"

"Now get out of my sight."

"Yes, Sarn't Major!"

♦

Two days later at the passing out parade we, the twelve survivors, were commissioned as Second Lieutenants in Her Majesty's New Zealand Army. Despite everything and our professed indifference we were proud enough of our new status. Shiny pips on our shoulders, our new badges of rank.

We all dispersed to reclaim our civilian lives. We swore to reunite annually. We never did, although I often thought, not of Tom, Roger, Mike and the others, but of Corporal Davis. I wondered when his birth date was. I wondered whose son he was; if being the son of a farmer, an accountant or a lawyer or a doctor or a successful business man might have made a difference. Kept him out of the army, steered him into a line of work more suited to his predilections.

I wondered at his small life ended by prejudice and malice as surely as if he'd been the target of a North Vietnamese sniper.

Listed as 'killed in action' his youth and innocence evaporated, like ours. Just another casualty of another unjust war.

♦　♦　♦

The Lonely Life of Charles

The first memory Charles could recall was the sweet face of his nanny, her eyes warm and loving as she drew the covers up almost over his head. He liked the feeling of security that remained after she had wished him 'good night, hope the fleas don't bite' as she tiptoed across the cavernous room to his bedroom door and clicked off the only light.

By the time Molly had gone down the four flights of back stairs to the servant's, now properly called 'staff,' kitchen Charles was asleep.

"Oh, the poor wee tot," Molly said to her workmates who were gathered around the long table snatching a cup of tea and having a chat. "All alone up there. No brothers or sisters to keep him company. And I bet his stuck-up mother won't go near him to read him a story or give him a kiss."

"Course she won't. Far too busy. They're out to the Hunt Ball tonight," offered Mabel the cook, or 'chef' as her employer, Lady Louise, liked to call her.

Charles didn't know he was a 'poor wee tot.' He had no concept of loneliness because he knew no different. As he grew older Molly sometimes said in tones of pity, "Aren't you lonely, Charley?"

Charles always replied, 'Don't know."

To his unformed understanding the names Molly, mummy and nanny sounded similar and became interchangeable in his mind. He had a vague understanding that Molly was his nanny and someone called mummy was someone else. He had no idea who the woman who called herself mummy was or what her role was in his young life.

Every evening at 5.30 a bell would ring which sent Molly into a spin.

"Come on, dear, hurry up," she would say as she whipped away the half-finished peaches and cream he'd been enjoying. "Time to go and say good night to mummy and daddy."

Charles would be cross at this abrupt end to his dinner. Molly, bless her, did her best to mollify him with the promise of a treat later. Nevertheless Charles's immediate irritation towards adults in general and 'mummy and daddy' in particular became a deep seated resentment.

Molly held his hand as she led him towards the dark wood-panelled double doors behind which mummy and daddy apparently lived because he had never seen them anywhere else in the house. He always felt a stab of fear when Molly let his hand go as the door swung open.

"Good evening, ma'am, sir." She curtsied perfunctorily, "Here is young master to say goodnight."

Molly pushed Charles forward.

The boy approached the tall woman holding a glass full of green liquid in one hand and a cigarette in an elegant holder in the other. As usual the man he was to address as 'daddy' was hiding his face behind a newspaper.

"Have you been a good boy today?"

The tall woman swirled the liquid around her glass.

"Yes, nanny, ah Molly," stammered Charles. The man rattled his newspaper which rattled Charles. "Oh, sorry. I meant mummy. Yes, I have been a good boy, mummy."

There was a silence as mummy and daddy scrutinised Molly who, much to his relief, stood by the open door, looking as though she wished she was elsewhere.

"Well," daddy harrumphed, "Good night then."

Molly rushed forward to grasp Charley's hand and hurried him out of the room.

Molly led him up to his bedroom even though he knew his way perfectly well and usually skipped on ahead. He sensed something was wrong with Molly and sure enough when she came to draw the covers up over his head just as he liked she said, "You must remember mummy and daddy love you even though they forgot to say so tonight."

171

Next morning his curtains were ripped open to let the light glare in. A loud voice screeched, "Hands off cocks and on to socks."

"Where's Molly?" cried a shocked Charles with no idea what the voice meant other than it sounded rude to his unsullied ears.

"Never you mind, Charley boy. I'm your nanny from now on. Don't forget it if you know what's good for you. Let's be having you now. Ten minutes to get down to the kitchen," commanded the nanny sounding like a parade ground drill sergeant to Charles's television informed eyes and ears.

♦

With the resilience of the very young Charles soon forgot about Molly. That sense of soft and loving security snatched away from him one morning faded from his memory as though he had known no other, as a harsher routine established itself. The strangers he knew as mummy and daddy said they loved him on the evenings he was taken in to see them. As always their words left him unmoved as he had no idea of what 'love' meant.

He did work out that this professed 'love' meant he had some leverage over his nannies. He never had a nice one after Molly and when he'd had enough of those who were downright horrible he accidentally on purpose called his mummy nanny or vice versa. The first time after losing Molly it was an accident brought on by the tension he felt whenever in his parent's presence. But that caused him to remember the circumstances of Molly's disappearance and he realised he was onto a good thing.

With his nannies disappearing every so often and the lack of interest from his parents that he perceived as indifference his feelings towards other people were atrophied if not stillborn. In short he grew up without any feelings whatsoever.

Except for his dog. His parents bought him a Border Collie puppy. His father had recalled his own intensely pleasant emotional reaction as a lad when a dog had turned up. He'd long accepted the wisdom of his parents who told him to 'harden up' when the pet had been run over by the Rolls Royce of a visiting royal. He persuaded mummy that a similar experience would do Charles no harm.

Charles named the puppy Maggie, which happened to be the name of the not too horrible nanny he had at the time. Which immediately got her fired by mummy, ever sensitive to her lack of maternal feelings yet envious of any feelings her son might reveal for another.

Charles and Maggie became inseparable. Although required to be discreet within the Manor House, the grounds of the estate were theirs to roam. Sometimes the two of them helped the shepherds with stock work. Maggie proved an excellent sheep dog and, with her master, built up something of a rapport with the farm workers.

When Charles came home for term breaks from boarding school Maggie would be waiting at the entrance to the grounds and run alongside the Bentley all the way to the Manor House, barking and cavorting. She did this for years until one holiday she wasn't there. Charles felt real emotion for the first time. He was eighteen and in his last year at boarding school. Maggie had died of old age.

Apart from his devotion to his dog Charles had grown up to be a selfish and self-absorbed young man. He could not sustain relationships with boys or girls. He did find it slightly easier to speak with girls than boys because he had been brought up by females. They soon tired of his indifference and transferred their attentions to livelier prospects.

The boys' boarding school he attended provided him with friends of a sort. But they were a far cry from the trustworthy farm and estate workers whom he privately thought of as friends even though he knew his parents would have been appalled at the notion.

As soon as he decently could after arriving home for the hols Charles whistled up Maggie and the two of them would make a mad rush for the sheep yards on the far side of the bottom sixty. Horace, the head shepherd, had his tied cottage right next to the yards. Horace always seemed pleased to see him and didn't mind listening to Charles prattle on about school as they drafted lambs. He was amused to notice that Charles clammed up whenever Irene, his daughter, the same age as Charles, arrived home after day school at the comprehensive in town.

Horace had the wisdom not to blanch when one day Charles told him, "I got six of the best last week for whacking my fag with a hockey stick."

Quietly horrified Horace asked, "Does much of that sort of thing go on then?"

"Oh yes," Charles replied. "And much worse besides. Bullying is nothing compared to the buggery. We're up each other all the time. Especially when a load of young ones come up to senior school."

"You don't think there's anything wrong with all that then?" Horace was unable to entirely keep the disapproval out of his voice.

"Well, no," said Charles as though considering for the first time that there could be anything questionable about any aspect of his life. "We all do it. Why should there be anything wrong with doing unto the weak what the strong had already done to us?"

He laughed as he parodied the biblical phrase.

Over the years of similar conversations with Horace he began to sense that buggery and bullying were not the norm and indeed frowned upon in some circles. Nevertheless by the time he left boarding school he was well-practised in both activities. Peer pressure and the desire to be accepted by any society however macabre won out over the morals of his friend who, after all, lived in such a different world and couldn't be expected to understand Charles's.

♦

To Horace's relief the slight attachment that had developed between Charles and his daughter Irene faded when Charles finally left home for Cambridge University. Once there he turned his whole attention to rugby. There was no place in his brutalized outlook for girls.

174

Focused on rugby his studies came a mediocre second. He did manage to keep up and pass enough papers to stay in the programme. Truth was he found the study of international finance rather dry. The excitement of clutching at the sweaty male body of an opposing prop or indeed a quick rogering by a willing team-mate was too much distraction.

The press were tedious in their endeavour to trap one of the upper class Oxbridge boys with their trousers down. Especially if it confirmed their view of the degeneracy of the supposed aristocracy.

Poor old Charles was the victim of a winger's need for cash to square off his dealer by selling him out to a pap. The snapper got him full frontal during what Charles thought was a bit of consensual hanky-panky in the away changing rooms. His picture in a comprising position behind a kneeling party who could not be identified was splashed across the front pages of the next day's tabloids.

The university could no more tolerate the publicity, even though the coaches had turned a blind eye, than Charles' parents could the shame. His account was frozen. He was out, uncapped, with few prospects although he did consider briefly professional rugby which would provide unfettered opportunities for indulging in unnatural acts. Never before faced with the dilemma of what to do next he called on Horace.

"I was shafted," Charles explained to Horace. "It was a set up for a bit of cash. For goodness sake, if the winger had asked me for money to pay off his dealer I would have given him some of daddy's."

"I believe you, son, but you must know by now I think you're heading down the wrong road."

"I do, Horace, but what shall I do now?"

"You've got to do something different. What are you, twenty-four? Your parents are about as wealthy as it is possible to be. Tap them for a bit of working capital and go into business for yourself."

"Those tightwads," Charles snorted. "I'm on the outer there, old chap. But if you think it worth it I'll give it a go."

Working through the estate bailiff Charles made an appointment to see his parents. He was made to wait outside the same imposing doors that had terrified him as a small boy, frightened of the two austere people who waited behind it to bid him 'goodnight.'

When eventually the bailiff opened the door and indicated he might enter, Charles was appalled that he should feel as intimidated as he had all those years ago.

"Mummy, daddy," he stammered. "Thank you for seeing me. I know you are not pleased with me at the moment, but it wasn't my fault."

"Hush, Charles. You brought shame on the family." Daddy spoke sternly. "That's enough. It doesn't matter whose fault it was."

"Look, mummy and daddy, I understand I've upset you with this but I've never been any trouble before. I have a plan to make something of myself and then perhaps you'll even notice me and be proud of me."

"We doubt it very much," his father growled.

"Could you possibly see your way to lending me some seed capital to get a business idea I have underway?"

"Bugger off," retorted daddy, shocked at the temerity of his son who yet was a stranger to him.

In the circumstances this was an unfortunate choice of phrase. Charles stormed out. He resolved to get revenge on what he now realised were the heartless people who had no claim to be his parents.

◆

Old Horace, now a widower, didn't mind Charles living with him on the estate. Charles said he needed a base with the estate address so that no-one would realise that he was estranged from his parents. Horace made sure his old friend the bailiff kept the parents in the dark about Charley's whereabouts.

"The only downside I can see," said Horace, as plain speaking as ever, "is that staying here with me will no doubt bring you into contact with Irene again. She often comes out on the weekend."

"Why should that be a problem, old mate?"

"Because she's married to a good bloke. They've got kids. My grandkids and I don't want you starting up any of that old hanky-panky now and upsetting the apple-cart."

"No need to worry. We were only ever friends. In case you didn't read the papers I really do bat for the other side although it's a rare innings these days. If you know what I mean?"

"I think I do." Horace was uncertain if he ever would truly understand. "That's all right then, lad," he added brightly as the meaning of Charles's explanation dawned.

◆

Charles set up his computer, scanner and printer in the front room of Horace's small cottage. This technological conversion of what had been a plain room intrigued Irene's twin boys. Soon enough, as proficient as Charles was and not at all convinced he needed help, they were helping Charles anyway to design posters, write letters, spread-sheet data and all the other jobs that go into launching a new enterprise.

He hatched a plan to go into the rock festival and alternative lifestyle promotion business.

When they needed a break they would drop over to the sheep yards and pitch in with whatever task was going. At first Irene or her husband or both, if they were around, were wary of his contact with their young boys. One day Charles said to Irene with a laugh, "Just because I'm a little bent doesn't mean I like kids that way, you know."

After a while, when it was clear Charley meant what he said, they relaxed.

He had not felt so content since the happy days when he and his old dog Maggie had helped with the work, although sometimes the sight of the twins playing with Maggie's descendants caused a nostalgic tug to his heart. This both surprised and pleased him because he had long ago assumed he didn't possess that organ.

He had to remind himself not to let his increasingly benevolent feelings towards the world in general reduce his desire for revenge against his parents.

◆

It seemed as though his and other public schools spawned a generation of anaemic, pouting, strutting, skinny boys considered losers fit only to be bullied by the rugby playing elite. By some inexplicable twist of fate many of these no-hopers displayed a talent for music of a sort never before heard of that appealed to the mass of under-educated youth.

Charles with his ingrained ruthless self-absorption threatened many of his old school chums, now rock stars, with tabloid exposure of past misdeeds to convince them that signing on for his rock festival was a good idea. Buggery, bullying and thuggery, whether perpetrator or victim, were all the same to him. He enlisted enough famous degenerate acts to attract a sell-out crowd of hopheads, drug addicts and generally spaced-out freaks. Then he sold the same number of tickets over again.

Horace and the estate staff kept Charles informed of his parents' movements and, anyway, he knew they generally spent the summer yachting on the Med. That year was no different.

Preparations complete, he opened the gates of the Manor House grounds to the rampant hordes. The punters were so appreciative in their spacy way they didn't notice the grossly overcrowded conditions or lack of facilities.

The house and grounds succumbed to the onslaught and, within hours of the first thrash metal band taking the stage, were trashed beyond belief. It didn't help that it rained during the afternoon turning the beautifully manicured lawns to mush. The rose gardens disappeared early in the show as the punters outdid each other to present a flower to the nearest pretty girl. Much of the herbage from the herb garden ended up being smoked with some swearing better hallucinogenic properties than marijuana.

All things considered Charles had a super day; made a lot of money and a few new friends. Irene and her physically intimidating husband looked after the money and made sure the acts, no matter how out of it they were, got paid folding money. The twins, despite their teenage years, assumed an authority that saw them step into the roles of stage managers who kept the show rolling. Horace and most of the estate workers including the bailiff acted as crowd control and general dispute resolvers and problem facilitators.

◆

Charles never found it necessary to respond to the invoices Mummy and Daddy sent him for the total renovation of the Manor House. He did, however, after the debrief a few days later call Horace into what was really his own front room, now known as Revenge HQ.

"Here's a little something for your trouble, my old friend."

Charles handed Horace a cheque for a large sum of money. "Help you get your house back to rights when I move out to our new office in town."

"No trouble at all, lad. It's been a pleasure," Horace choked back a tear. "I'll miss you. We will all miss you."

"Now, now, old man, don't go gooey on me. This isn't the end of the story you know," Charley laughed. "Anyway look here's a cheque for Irene and Bill. Maybe for the boys' education although for Christ's sake don't let her send them to my old school."

◆

Charles had found his metier. The Manor House Rock Festival went down in history as the first really successful event of its type. He went on to promote many successful rock festivals, using his first as a template; grossly overcrowded, minimal facilities, liberal rules and great acts in the grounds of country houses usually belonging to, or inherited from, the parents of his old school chums shy of adverse publicity.

His most recent double sold–out event was 'Ruck 'n Maul Aid' from which a small percentage was paid to the charity devoted to the care of AIDS-infected or brain damaged rugby players.

Charley's largesse helped the twins through their schooling, but their working class origins steered them inevitably into the army. Both qualified as officers, Garry in the Engineers Regiment, Mark with the Second Battalion, The Duke of Lancaster's Regiment. Both were killed within three days of each other in Helmund Province. The pity of it was that both were on short commissions due to leave at the end of the mission to help Charley in the global business that had grown too big for him.

At the funeral he looked in vain for mummy and daddy who he thought might have paid their respects to the daughter and grandsons of their longest serving farm worker. Revenge long dormant as his motivation, surfaced briefly to be quashed by reason as he turned his attention to helping the living.

Occasionally his picture of a man saddened by but accepting of the vicissitudes of life appears in the press, usually the Telegraph, or on TV promoting this or opening that, always accompanied by two or three dogs, always border collies.

◆　◆　◆

Heights of Accomplishment

On a beautiful autumn day in late September Jack Warburton lifted the old girl off from Mepal climbing out over Ely Cathedral heading due east towards Germany and Berlin. Jack had done this trip many times before but never in daylight and never without bombs and never with such a light heart. The summer stretched on as though the weather gods knew the world was at last at peace and gave the world weather to match.

Three months after the end of the war in Europe, suddenly it was over everywhere. The unwelcome prospect of doing to the Japanese what the RAF had recently been doing to the Germans was no more. Almost to his disbelief, but immense relief, Jack had survived and his crew with him.

Aircrew were being demobbed. Married personnel had already gone. His old crew had sailed on the Royal Mail Ship *Andes* with most of 75 Squadron on their way back to New Zealand. Jack was one of the few aircrew detailed to remain behind to hand Mepal back to the RAF. He was left to wander around the base as lost as a schoolboy left behind while the rest of the school went on holiday. Lancasters, that a short time ago were pampered like babies and loved as winged chariots with human personalities, had begun to accumulate forlornly around the hardstands, parked forgotten and unappreciated.

Jack, bored kicking his heels on Mepal base, was glad to be tasked to fly with a scratch crew to Berlin's Templehoff airfield to pick up some freight. Of his new crew only Frank Williams, the radio operator, was known to him. Frank was, like Jack, a veteran of uncountable ops and just as reticent. The engineer and navigator, whose names meant nothing to him, were straight out of aircrew training and had no combat experience.

Bomb aimer and gunners, ammunition and bombs were no longer needed, making the aircraft feel light and even skittish to Jack as he gained height. It was as though the old girl knew the burden of war had been lifted as she responded like a Spitfire to Jack's every subtle move on the controls.

As soon as they overflew the coastal beacon on the Norfolk coast Frank wedged himself comfortably in his seat behind the bulkhead that housed the communication panel and said, "Wake me if you need me, Skipper" - and went immediately to sleep.

This made the two rookies nervous and one of them asked Jack if he should wake up the radio operator. Seeing that Frank still had one earphone on and accustomed to how his previous operator had an uncanny ability to instantly come to life if their call sign was transmitted, Jack shook his head.

More out of habit, because the need was long gone, Jack took the old girl up until she started to wallow in the thin air as she reached her ceiling nearly five miles above the hazy blue of the English Channel. Height to him was like sea room to a sailor; space and time, the more the better, to be guarded and conserved for the time if the unthinkable happened, when the flak or a Schrage Musik equipped night fighter found them to rake the Lanc's vulnerable belly with cannon fire.

But there was no unthinkable to happen now so Jack just let her float along for a while, ignoring the uneasy glances of the two rookies. Then he spotted some towering cumulus ahead and below and put her into a shallow dive aiming straight for it. He skidded and hauled the old girl around the cloud, diving in and out like a dolphin through waves. Jack knew this might be his last chance to have some fun and somehow the old girl knew it too.

He rolled her on to her starboard wing then flicked her over to port, diving then climbing, more like a fighter plane than a 30-ton bomber. The navigator started to sweat trying to keep them on track. Jack wasn't worried; he almost knew the compass bearings to Berlin and back by heart and, anyway, as long as they didn't wander too far off track, Berlin would be hard to miss in daylight. When he thought back to how he used to fling the fully-laden bomber violently around with a night fighter on their tail he smiled at the rookies' concern. The engineer had never witnessed extreme aerobatics in a heavy bomber before and was worried about oil surges, but Jack just said, "She'll be right;" and she was.

Approaching the outer perimeter of Templehoff Jack asked the navigator to give Frank a nudge. He came instantly awake and remarked, as though he'd never been asleep, "Quiet trip then," as a statement of fact. The navigator and engineer looked at each other in disbelief.

Jack asked Frank to call for landing instructions and soon they rolled to a stop outside the hangars. Nobody on the ground seemed to expect them or know why they were there until eventually a ground erk detailed the driver of a lorry with a tarpaulin-covered load to start loading the Lancaster.

♦

To carry the load the bomb bay doors had to be closed which meant loading through the main hatch at the rear of the fuselage. Jack could see this was going to take forever if he and the crew didn't lend a hand. Even so some of the larger crates labelled 'Surplus Ordinance' had to be jemmied open and the contents, clearly booty looted from the recently defeated, manhandled into the old girl's interior.

Tunics discarded, sweating in the sun loading the crates, Jack looked at Frank and asked, "What do you think of this then, mate?"

"About as much as you," Frank replied. "This isn't right and it's against regs as well. Some bastards getting rich at these poor people's expense and we're doing the donkey work."

"Well, it's nearly loaded so we'll just have to go along with it for now," said Jack. "Anyway if we don't get moving it'll be dark by the time we get back to Blighty."

Just as the navigator and engineer tumbled out of the hatch to report the load was secure a jeep with Pay Corps insignia drew up with an Army Major in the passenger seat. The desk jockey type with an immaculately tailored uniform, European theatre ribbons notably absent, Army of Occupation flashes conspicuous.

"Be careful with my property, you chaps." Unaware he was speaking to air force officers as he added pompously, "Got to teach these German beggars a lesson, you know, what?"

Jack turned away contemptuously, catching Frank's eye, whose expression mirrored his own. Both men had seen and been at least partly responsible for the destruction wrought upon the German people. The unspoken thought felt by both was that those poor misguided people had been taught enough of a lesson.

By dusk, much later than Jack had hoped, they were refuelled and cleared for takeoff. The *joie de vivre* Jack felt on the outbound flight had evaporated. The others were quiet too. Frank didn't go to sleep this time, but glared moodily at his radio panel sometimes muttering angrily to himself or to controllers as they cleared the aircraft across Germany then Holland.

On takeoff and climb-out towards the west Jack felt the controls were a little sluggish, which he put down to the weight of the contraband, although he knew bomb loads had been much heavier. Rather than tax the old girl he relaxed his golden rule of going for height and let her amble along at an easy 7000 feet.

Frank noticed at once and over the intercom asked, "Not going for height, skip?"

"Nah, Frank, she doesn't seem to want to."

Jack knew the other two listening on the intercom would think him a bit strange implying the aircraft had human wants. He also knew Frank would twig straight away.

As Jack settled the autopilot down into the monotony of the flight, with no need to stay vigilant against the threat of attack, the drone of the Merlin engines mesmerised him into reverie. He thought about Frank and how surprised he was to find himself warming to him and the easy way they had with each other. The war had taught him to have no friends. Friends got the chop. His old crew were in awe of him, but they weren't friends. They were in awe of his luck that always brought them back. With this crushing burden of expectation he could no more be friends with them than anyone else.

He knew it wasn't only luck that let them survive. It was survival learnt from experience and the cold cunning coming from the overriding sense of self-preservation that all the old hands had. He had learnt to take from the pre-op briefing that which would give him an edge; to use the information to his advantage even if it exposed other less experienced crews to slightly more risk. He told no one of this, not even the other six members of his crew and they, in turn, recognised their survival depended on him alone and said nothing although they surely noticed.

Even if he was slotted to take off early, once airborne, he let the old girl drift back to the middle of the stream to seek safety in numbers. To him it seemed less likely that the radar-controlled searchlights could single out the old girl to cone them for the heavy ack-ack. The German night fighters picked off the edges of the stream, avoiding the concentrated defence of the middle. Whatever height he was briefed to fly at he always gradually eased the laden Lanc up to above the main bomber stream. He had seen many aircraft hit by the falling bombs from friendly aircraft. Once the bomb aimer called 'bombs gone' and he'd flown straight and level for the agonising seconds it took for the photo flash to fire, Jack put the nose down to increase airspeed for the homeward leg.

The crackle of the intercom interrupted his reverie as the navigator announced, "Ten miles to the Dutch coast, skipper."

Jack looked down at the lights of Holland thinking how different it looked from the last time he had flown over enemy held territory in the dark. Then, the flashes of their exploding bombs amid the glare of the already blazing inferno passed beneath them unreeling like a silent horror movie. From the great height from which they bombed they could hear nothing except the roar of the engines and the slipstream. The occasional rattle of shrapnel from an exploding ack-ack shell against the fuselage told him the old girl was still appearing on German radar far below.

Usually on the bombing run Jack didn't look out. He wound his seat down so he could only see his instruments to concentrate on keeping the old girl steady until the bomb aimer reported 'bombs gone.' Anyway, he had seen many burning cities and one looked much like another.

He wound his seat down now; the peaceful lights of Holland reminded him of things he didn't want to be reminded of. The autopilot would keep her steady.

As they crossed the Dutch coast the engineer came up on the intercom, "Oil pressure on the starboard outer dropping, skipper,"

Jack ordered him to cut fuel and power to that engine and feather the prop. He had brought the old girl home on three engines many times. Apart from a few less knots of airspeed it hardly made any difference. All the same he regretted not going for height from the outset. Too late now.

A minute or so later Frank came up to report that his radios had gone dead and he would start check procedures to see if he could isolate the fault. Privately he thought 'fat chance.'

Committed now to the sea crossing Jack hoped nothing else would fail. He mused that the old girl liked carrying contraband no more than he. His musing put him in mind of how he thought of her as the 'old girl.' He had wanted to name her officially 'Old Girl,' but knew that it would invite derisive comment from others in the squadron. Plus the crew would never go for such an unglamorous name. So she remained the Lancaster with no name, no pin-up painted on her nose. Now and again one of the crew would pester him to have the squadron artist paint them a glamour-puss on the nose but he always dismissed the idea with a derisory, "What for? We'll probably get the chop soon anyway."

Again wrenched back to the present by the engineer's panicked voice, "Skipper, you won't bloody believe this, the port inner's lost oil pressure now as well."

Stifling his unease, Jack told him to go through the same procedures as before. Now they were down to two engines, over water, at night with no radio contact. Jack swore silently to himself for breaking his self-imposed height rule that had served him well so many times in the past. With two engines feathered the rate of sink, negligible before, began to increase. At least with an engine out on each side she was reasonably stable and flying straight. If both had been out on the same side Jack doubted he could have held her straight for so long. The crabbing would have scrubbed off more speed and the sink increased.

Jack tried trimming her slightly nose down to increase airspeed and therefore maintain altitude. But it was as though she didn't want to be trimmed. He who had been in control in the most harrowing situations suddenly had the despairing feeling that a greater force was at work. He kept this to himself.

Frank, with nothing to do, his radios dead for no explicable reason that he could find, came up and crouched behind Jack's seat. He watched Jack try every trick he knew to get the aircraft to fly right. Frank leaned forward, lifted Jack's earphone bypassing the intercom so the others couldn't hear, and said, "She knows."

Jack twisted in his seat, smiled grimly at Frank and nodded. More to give the navigator something to do, Jack asked him to work out what were their chances of making land. Shortly the nav came back and with a catch in his voice said, "Skipper, with our current rate of sink and ground speed we'll hit the water about five miles short of the Norfolk coast. What the hell are we going to do?"

"Keep calm for a start and see if you can get a star fix. It might be handy to know where we are."

That would keep the young man busy.

Ditching within sight of the coast wouldn't be so bad in daylight but at night no one would see them and with no radio contact no-one would even know, let alone look for them. Mepal would assume they had stayed overnight in Berlin. It might be a few days before search and rescue were alerted.

Jack and Frank discussed their options, limited as they were, over the intercom not bothering to conceal the seriousness of their plight. Better the rookies should know the worst. They decided ditching, while they still had some height, power and control, was the only option. Next they needed a ship to ditch near so began looking out for lights in the pitch black void. But first they decided to lighten the aircraft by jettisoning the load. Maybe that would keep them airborne long enough to get them a bit closer to the coast.

Just as they made this decision the engineer screeched over the intercom, "Jesus Christ, the hydraulic pressure's gone! The flipping main gear lowered itself! Now what?"

"Get a grip man," commanded Jack coolly. "I'm working on it."

Jack immediately felt the drag effect on the controls of the lowered undercarriage, like being hauled up by powerful brakes. He and Frank *really* looked at each other now. Both knew what this meant.

"The old girl doesn't want us to ditch," said Jack.

"Yeah, skip," agreed Frank, "she's onto us all right. Ditching with the wheels down is curtains for us all. Even if we don't cartwheel she'll fill up faster than we can get out."

"You're going to have to bail out now while there's still a chance."

Jack spoke quietly and calmly. He knew he had little chance of escape himself. "Forget jettisoning the load, it won't make much difference now."

Frank and the other two crew clipped on their chutes and made their way down to the forward escape hatch. Frank turned the jettison handle, but nothing happened. He kicked it and still it didn't budge. Frank motioned for the crew to follow him to the main hatch in the rear. All three of them heaved on the handle, but that didn't budge either. Cross, and for the first time a little afraid, Frank whirled around to grab the axe placed for just such an emergency to find the bracket empty. It was gone!

Assuming a slack pre-flight check, he cursed as he made his way back up to the cockpit to find Jack wrestling with the stick trying to keep the old girl level while the others jumped. Frank realised then that Jack would have no chance to get out once he let go of the controls. Centrifugal forces would trap him as surely as if he had been tied into his seat. A great wave of sorrow came over him as he saw Jack's predicament.

But three of them still had a chance and they must take it. Frank reported that they couldn't bail out through either escape hatch so were going to go out through the bomb bay doors, which they would have to open manually. Jack nodded, not looking at Frank; not letting him see that he, too, knew he was doomed.

Alone again in the cockpit struggling with all his strength at the controls even now Jack could not think badly of the old girl. It wasn't her fault. Once the others had jumped maybe he would let her spiral in and take him with her. Nobody would miss him; nobody would grieve. He smiled grimly at the irony of surviving war then ending like this. He thought briefly of his father and mother waiting far away for him to return.

Crouched on the narrow walkway above the bomb bay Frank and the other two began the laborious task of winding open the huge bomb bay doors that ran almost the whole length of the underside of the Lanc. Soon crates began to fall away as the doors inched wider. Cameras, diamonds, binoculars, jewellery, gold, silver, bullion, priceless objects glittered and flashed as they tumbled out into the slipstream. Millions of pounds worth of looted treasure cascaded down into black oblivion.

They crouched, mesmerised by the sight even as they should have been clambering down to follow into the void.

"Hold on a minute, chaps," came Jack's disembodied voice over the intercom. They froze, poised on the edge of the walkway, seconds away from jumping.

"Frank you'd better come up and have a look at this."

Cursing and almost weeping, certain that this delay meant the end for them all, but unwilling to leave Jack alone, Frank made his way forward again. As he passed the radio operator's panel he was amazed to see it lit up, live and blinking.

"You're not going to believe this. I think the old girl is going to forgive us. Look!" Jack pointed at the engineer's instrument panel. "Look at the oil pressures." The needles were flickering. "Get that engineer up here pronto. Set those props to coarse; let's see if we can breathe some life into those Merlins."

First the port inner caught then the starboard outer, roughly at first like smokers clearing their throats. Then both engines evened out as smoothly as ever. The crew cheered and hollered like excited children. Jack felt the extra lift immediately and the altimeter stopped unwinding.

The puzzled but happy engineer reported to Jack.

"Oil pressures are back to normal and I don't believe this, but hydraulic pressure is coming up too. Do you want to raise the gear and close the doors, skipper?"

"Do I?" yelled Jack. "Of course I do!"

As soon as the green lights for 'closed and locked' blinked Jack pushed all four throttles hard open against the stops. That lovely old warhorse lifted her nose like a thoroughbred scenting home and surged for the loom of the lights of the Norfolk coast.

Soon Frank had them cleared to land. This time Jack wound his seat right up so he could see the lights, dark for so long now bright and clear, of the city of Ely and the nearby villages twinkling away across the flat fens of East Anglia. As he lined up for the approach the welcoming lights of Mepal's main runway stretched away in front of him etching an image into his brain that he knew would remain forever. A beautiful sight that during the long, dark wartime years he had often thought he would never live to see.

Jack landed perfectly, touching down on all three. He wasn't sure if it was his skill or the old girl's. She had never been so responsive. Maybe she already knew Jack had decided this was to be their last flight. He wanted to leave it at that; it was enough. Time to move on. He would speak to the CO in the morning; see if he could bring his demob forward.

As they clambered out of the rear hatch Frank looked at the bracket where the axe should have been. There it was, plain as day! He turned and looked at Jack and they shrugged at each other as if to say, "Well I'll be blowed."

They burst out laughing to the puzzlement of the two rookies.

As the crew walked away from the huge aircraft Jack turned and looked back at her. Everything about her reeked of war, to kill people, wreck, destroy and maim. Yet as far as Jack was concerned she was a thing of beauty doing exactly what was right and true. Besides, she had kept him and his crew alive, even though she had exercised a bit of moral judgement right at the end as though she too had had enough. Although he knew in his heart of hearts that the old girl was only a mass of plastic, oil, metal, rubber and glass, he felt more strongly for her than he had for any aircraft or, in fact, human being since the war began.

Jack turned back to catch up with the others and saw Frank had waited and been watching him, concerned for him. Jack's rigid self-control, imposed for all those wartime years faltered, as he realised the need was over. In a moment of insight he knew that because of what he and Frank had shared that night, the countless terrors they had endured on all the other nights with different aircraft and crews, for the first time he could make a friend, be a friend.

He slung his arm over Frank's shoulder.

"Come on, mate. I'll buy you a beer."

They walked slowly as though with all the time in the world, all their lives to be lived ahead of them, towards the welcoming lights of the mess.

Beers on the table between them Jack leaned forward to light Frank's cigarette and said, "Ever thought it would be possible to put fertiliser on by air?"

♦

Epilogue

Jack Warburton was 24-years old when the Second World War ended. He had been a Flying Officer, pilot in command, 75(NZ) Squadron RAF for almost two years at war's end. As well as stints as an instructor in heavy bomber conversion units he had completed two tours of operations.

He, like most in the RAF at the end of the war in Europe, was preparing to transfer to the Japanese theatre. It was especially satisfying to him that it was air bombardment that brought World War 2 to a sudden, unexpected end.

Jack did see his CO the next day, but although he never flew the old girl again, indeed she was scrapped as a worn-out warhorse within weeks, he wasn't discharged until the middle of 1946. Although rather miffed at this at the time, his duties were light and untaxing. He came to see this as a stroke of luck as by January 1946 he had met and married the daughter of a local farmer. He spent every weekend and all of his leaves on his father-in-law's large farm revelling in the flat landscapes and huge open skies of the fens.

During this time his ideas on aerial top dressing germinated and with the connivance of his in-laws and the air force he learnt a lot, mostly by trial and error using the squadron's surplus light aircraft.

After their Berlin flight Jack wasn't to see Frank for almost a year. Frank mysteriously obtained his discharge only a few days after that flight and was home in New Zealand before Christmas 1945. He married his childhood sweetheart, and soon after they had a baby daughter.

Jack and his wife arrived in New Zealand in September 1946.

Jack and Frank had kept in touch. Both could see that the idea of aerial topdressing, born of a flippant remark and nurtured by Jack's experiments in England, was good. They recognised the irony of their desire to still try and bomb the earth, albeit with a rather more peaceful intent.

Their partnership started in the late southern spring of 1946 with one war-surplus Tiger Moth working in the central North Island. The rest is history.

Their first Tiger was named 'Old Girl' painted proudly on her nose. Thereafter there was always at least one 'Old Girl' in the fleet at any one time.

♦

Dedicated to my late father who flew as a radio operator with 75 (New Zealand) Squadron RAF from Mepal, Cambridgeshire, during 1945. In September 1945, as a 22 year old Warrant Officer, he was repatriated on the RMS *Andes* back to New Zealand where he greeted his war bride who arrived in January 1946.

♦   ♦   ♦

Wahines

I used to want to be like my old man. I would have said 'loved' by him, but that's a bit strong for any kid. Maybe I might come to that later on after I'd had a taste of real love with a sheila or maybe a kid of my own. That was before he drowned.

My father was a fisherman. He owned a skiff that had a diesel inboard that chugged away, stinking to high heaven. Probably why the old bugger smoked forty a day; dilute the stink of diesel fumes and rotting fish in the bilge.

He'd named the boat 'Wahine' after his missus, he said, my mother. His mates ribbed him about the inter-island ferry 'Wahine' that sank coming into Wellington Harbour in 1968. Though even if the real Wahine hadn't sunk it would probably have been scrapped by now.

His mates called him Ed or Eddy. He was Edward to my mother, usually. 'Bastard' after he disappeared.

The boat was more than one man could manage. Thing was, nobody would go out with him so he had no option. Said he preferred to be alone at sea anyway, so it wasn't any skin off his nose.

He was never without a fag hanging out of the corner of his mouth. He lit the next from the last. Mother nagged him about it; said the coffin nails would be hammered into the lid of his death box one day soon. His denial usually ended in a fit of coughing and hawking gobs into the sandy grass in front of our house.

"Rubbish," he said. "The sea will get me first."

He was right. One day he didn't come back. He went off alone in his skiff as usual. My mother nagged him about that too. She said going out to sea on your own was as stupid as smoking forty a day if you wanted to live.

My father, I can see now, wasn't a happy man. Around the house anyway. Maybe he was when he was out fishing. He went out often enough so I guess he must have been.

When he didn't come back one evening with the wind getting up and the surf crashing on the main beach my mother said she knew it, he was a fool going out on his own. My father was right, too; the sea did get him first. So they were both right so then I suppose they were both happy. Mum was happy because she didn't have to nag my father anymore and I'm guessing my father was happy because he always was when he was out at sea and now he always would be.

The only living person who came out worse from all this was me. My mother started to notice my shortcomings, apparently many, and nagged me just as she had nagged her missing husband. I began to understand why the old man took off out of the house as much as he did.

Even though I was a normal self-obsessed teenager then, when he disappeared I suspected my old man of trickery. I half expected Wahine to chug around the point at the head of the harbour in a cloud of black diesel. Then his mates on the wharf would shout at him, "Long time no see sea, Eddie," accompanied by raucous laughter at their own wit.

Wahine never chugged round the point again, nor anywhere for all I knew. The hope he was playing a trick faded to the certainty he had drowned, which is what everybody else thought anyway. Maybe he'd had a coughing fit from chain-smoking and fallen overboard.

After a suitable time my mother organised a memorial service, remembrance service, the vicar called it. We couldn't have a funeral because there was no body. But the coroner pronounced him dead long after the official search was abandoned. No trace of him or his boat was found. I was the only one who cared about him, even though I'd come to hate him too for karking out on me. My mother wasn't too upset. She'd long since given up on him ever showing any interest in her.

Funnily enough, even though I'd hardly ever been out with him because my mother said it was too dangerous, I became interested in the sea enough to make marine studies my major. Conservation was my thing and often as part of a research project I would be down at the dock gathering catch data or inspecting specimen fish.

One day I was on the wharf where all the fishing boats dock and a Samoan guy off one of the big deep sea trawlers that sometimes refuel up in the islands came over to me and asked if I was Eddy's son. I was a bit surprised because by then the old man had been missing for nearly twenty years. Yeah, now and again something reminded me of him, like every damn anniversary of the ferry sinking rehashed on the TV news or maybe the passing smell of an old boat. Sure, my rancour at his sudden disappearance had long since gone. But it was a long time since I'd heard his name mentioned by my mother or his mates let alone a stranger.

I looked sharply at the Samoan to see if he was pulling my leg about my father's Wahine or any of the other things that had become minor legends, but were probably typical fishermen's tall tales. He looked serious enough so I admitted I was Eddy's son.

The Samoan said he had a message for me which was to tell the boy that he and his mother were wrong. The Samoan guy would say no more; not even who exactly had given him the message nor confirm that it was from my father. Said he didn't know, had no idea, why should he?

It took me a while to work out what it all meant. Eventually I figured out that the old man must still be alive. I kept it from my mother. She had taken up with a boisterous little fellow who owned a grocery shop down the road, seemed to enjoy being nagged and definitely didn't smoke and hated fishing.

It wasn't difficult to trace the route of the Samoan's trawler's last voyage. The companies were pretty used to me poking around for information and as long as it wasn't too sensitive, like fishing co-ordinates or landed prices, they mostly co-operated.

It wasn't unusual for me to embark on a trawler for research as long as the department approved. I still wasn't sure if I wanted to find my father after such a long time. My vision of him was from when I was a teenager; maybe he was nothing like I imagined him to be.

I decided to go with the flow. If I could make a legitimate research case, which was a given, embark on a fishing vessel heading up to the islands with a convivial skipper then I would let serendipity make the decision for me.

As luck would have it the big deep sea trawler Seaswirl docked to replenish within a couple of days of me making my case with the department. Tony the skipper and his first mate Jimbo were pleased to have some company, especially as I'd been with them before. They'd spent a fair bit of time trawling the southern ocean and were looking forward to the warmer temperatures of the deep Tongan Trench and Samoan Basin. The law required I sign on as a deckhand, which as an academic always made me feel proud, like being one of the crew.

A couple of days out, with the fishing conversation running dry, I confided my half-hatched parental search agenda to the two officers. I showed them a copy of the Samoan's trawler's track and Tony said, 'No problem.' Turned out he and Jimbo had an option on a long-liner and were considering going out on their own with the backing of some rich investors. On what might be their last voyage for Seaswirl's owners they were not worried about the consequences of costing their present employer a little time.

It wasn't clear from the copy of the trawler's track whether it had called in to Asau Harbour on the north western side of Samoa's Savai'i Island, but it went close and was the only harbour deep enough to take either the Samoan's trawler or Seaswirl. Tony reckoned obtaining fresh fruit from the locals was a legitimate reason for tying up for an hour or two.

"Take as long as you want," he laughed, then slightly more serious, "as long as you're back in a couple of hours."

Asau Harbour had seen better days. But there were signs its glory days might return, not from farming or fishing but from tourists. Workmen were sweating on the foundations of a large new resort underway on the far side of the village.

It seemed as though nearly everyone who lived in the village had come down to the wharf to watch Seaswirl tie up. Many had produce for sale and they were excited to welcome this unusual visitor. Once I'd disembarked I spoke to a distinguished-looking gentleman observing the activity with good humour.

"Has another trawler maybe not so big as Seaswirl visited recently?"

"Yes," he said in perfect English. "They had some problem with a pump and a part had to be flown up from Apia."

He seemed knowledgeable so I took a chance and asked, "Is there a pakeha named Ed or Eddy living nearby?"

"Of course. Everyone knows Eddy." He pointed me towards the beach and said, "Go along there and you will find him."

I wandered along the beachfront, heart thumping now that the moment of reunion might be near. After such a long time I was still not expecting to find the old man. As I walked along the beach leaving the bustle of activity around the wharf behind I was struck by the gentle pace of life. An occasional ramshackle vehicle raised some dust from the road that ran parallel to the beach but mostly people walked, ambling along as though with all the time in the world.

Without exception everyone who passed and noticed me on the beach raised their hand and called a greeting. One young man on a rusty bicycle yelled out, "Tolafa, Eddy's son."

This brought me up short. How did that fellow know? He was heading *towards* the wharf where the only hint I might have given of my purpose was to the distinguished gentleman.

Rounding a small headland revealed another beach, smaller than the one I'd just left and completely hidden from the village and wharf where Seaswirl was berthed. I walked on splashing through the warm shallows until I spotted a house built a little way back from the beach. The house was weather-beaten but solid of timber and iron. A covered deck the full width of the front faced the beach.

Sitting in a rusty deckchair was my old man. Even though I thought I was prepared for this, I was astounded. He had hardly aged in the twenty years. I stood as though embedded in the sand. He must have known it was me because he gestured for me to

198

come on up the path through the grass and palms. I wondered how he knew it was me. Even if he hadn't changed I had; from a 14-year old boy to a man.

As I left the beach I looked for the name on a tinny drawn up above the tide line, half-expecting to see 'Wahine II,' but it had no name. As I approached the house I was further surprised when a comely wahine came out with a gourd and poured whatever was in it into a coconut cup my father held out. Then she gave him an affectionate kiss born of familiarity, waved to me and went back inside.

I approached my father and he seemed unsurprised to see me.

"G'day, son," he said. "Come and meet your family."

With that a couple of brown kids, teenagers almost, came out of the house and stood shyly behind my father's deckchair.

"Meet your half brother and sister."

I was speechless. Recovering I asked, "How did you know I was coming?"

"Cell phone." He pointed to a Nokia I hadn't noticed on the deck beside his chair.

I laughed. I should have known.

Turned out Ed (I couldn't think of him as the 'old man' anymore) had been married island style to his wahine for a fair while. He'd been fishing north east of the Karikari Peninsular almost out of sight of the low coastline when Wahine's engine finally coughed to a stop. Luckily a Tongan long-liner passed within hailing distance on her way home. From Pangai in the Tongan Islands where the trawler ended her voyage Ed eventually worked his passage to Samoa intending to fly home from Apia. Asau was as far as he got, seduced by the place and his wahine, Talia.

She came and stood with their children behind Ed's chair and draped her arms fondly around his neck. She smiled almost as shyly as the children and said in beautifully Polynesian-accented English, "Welcome to Samoa, Eddy's son; you are my son now too."

I looked at them; a picture of a contented family. I noticed he wasn't coughing or smoking.

199

"I've given up. Too much to live for," he said, a little apologetically as he realised what he was implying was that I hadn't been worth living for before he disappeared.

Any remaining rancour buried deep within me born of rejection and abandonment evaporated. How could I resent this man who said that he left not because of me or even his wife, my mother? His leaving was just one of those things, serendipitous for him. He hadn't cared for his wife and he knew that was mutual. But he was glad to hear she'd found another bloke and laughed with me when I described the little weasel.

The hurting of me had disturbed him for years. But he didn't know what he could do about that without making it worse. Eventually he realised he needed to make peace with himself just as much as he needed to with me. That was why he'd seized the chance to make contact when the Samoan's trawler had called in unexpectedly. He'd heard through the mysterious way rumours fly around the ocean to the remote islands that poke their peaks above water that I'd done well. He laughed and held up his Nokia when he said this.

Talia plied me with raw fish marinated in coconut cream, which was delicious.

Samaria, her niece, turned up on a motor scooter. She was on holiday from her nurse's job in Apia. She was as beautiful and engaging as Talia must have been and pretty much still was, although not shy at all. Strangely, momentarily, I suddenly was.

As we laughed and joked, filling in the missing years I was being seduced. For a glorious minute I wondered if I too should or could make a life for myself in this beautiful harbour.

Faintly from far away, as though not wishing to completely spoil my reverie, the deep sound of Seaswirl's siren wafted above the bird call. I glanced at my watch prepared to be annoyed, but was surprised to see that nearly four hours had passed; way above the two I'd agreed with Tony. The skipper, clearly mindful of the tide, needed to cast off.

I took my leave without tears or sadness, hugging Ed for the first time in my life and laughing when he said he hoped it wouldn't be the last. Talia did cry a little bit and the kids who had soon got over their shyness shed a tear as well.

I'd left my goodbyes to the nurse until last. I was surprised at how gauche I felt for a thirty–four year old man. I decided to shake her hand politely, but she was having none of that and embraced me and brushed my lips with hers.

"See you soon," she said matter of factly as though it had been discussed and settled.

Taking her lead I nodded and said deadpan, "I've got a strong feeling I'd be needing hospital care in Apia very soon."

To which she laughed with me and said, "Nothing too serious I hope."

"Oh yes, very serious. Probably terminal."

As Seaswirl neared the harbour entrance I could see through the binoculars my new family standing on their beach waving and waving. Tony sounded the siren in short blasts which set off another bout of frantic waving.

I handed the glasses to Tony and then Jimbo.

"Lucky bugger," they said.

I'd gone looking for my father and found him. I'd found myself too, and also something totally unexpected.

♦　♦　♦

John Mack

About The Author

John Mack has been writing and editing for trade and club publications for many years. Since 2008 he has been Bay of Plenty correspondent for New Zealand Classic Car magazine. He is a graduate of Whitireia (Wellington) Polytechnic's Creative Writing course and has had stories published by Rural Women New Zealand in their *Ragwort and Thistles* collection of short stories about women on the land and The New Zealand Society of Authors (Bay of Plenty) in their Tauranga Memories collection.

www.johnmack.co.nz

www.ingramcontent.com/pod-product-compliance
Lightning Source LLC
Chambersburg PA
CBHW070928250626
47159CB00009B/3167